The Wishing Bones

GW00382069

Melody Fisher

CONTENTS

CHAPTER ONE

19th May 1536, the day that vicious, vindictive and manipulative creature will have to answer to God for the crimes committed against my King, my country and my family. Rumour has it that the King has already a replacement. Does Anne remember what it was like to be the chosen one, whilst her predecessor is cast out, deserted by those whom you thought cared? Does the new favourite give a second thought to Anne, or is she as self-centered and ruthless in her ambition to become the Queen and in its wake destroy the trust and abuse the love of the King, just as Anne has done.

I wish I could be present to witness the end of this woman. She cared not for anyone around her apart from her daughter and used her wiles, her influence and charm to bring down great people. The King's trusted friend from boyhood, Thomas More was executed because he could not bring himself to go against his beliefs. Thomas Wolsey, who served the King for years, was used until he turned from her and was it not for dying naturally, would have been executed also. Her hands are covered in blood and she is responsible for the execution of many, including her own brother.

I knew her long ago, before the titles, the ambition and the carefully calculated steps. I remember both her and her sister Mary. I spent most of my time in the herb garden and fields surrounding Hever, their childhood home. When not being carefully watched I could indulge myself playing games pretending to be the owner of the big house not just the offspring of an employee. I was roughly the same age as Anne and we used to play together when I didn't have chores to do. I can still smell the fragrant plants as we ran past them playing chasing games. This was all before she went to France. Back then she was still nice, still friendly and a happy girl to be around.

"Season, Season, hurry up with those herbs, I haven't got all day!" Mother was calling, I'd gone out to collect the list of ingredients mother had wanted from the garden and got distracted by Mistress Anne, she was showing me a spider's web and the efforts of the spider to repair it. Anne kept breaking the threads but the spider didn't give up, it was relentless in its perseverance and just kept repairing the damage.

I ran indoors with my basket of herbs. Mother was making a poultice as Lady Elizabeth Boleyn was suffering from a headache. My mother, Agnes, could make all manner of compresses, poultices and bindings to help with all ailments. Lady Elizabeth relied on her and mother had been with her for many more than the seven years that I had walked the earth. My mother had helped when Mistress Mary had been born, there had been other children apart from Mary, Anne and George but they had not survived, Lady Elizabeth said it was down to Agnes's skills that she had delivered a healthy child, when my mother had been absent things had not gone so well.

When I was born, around the same time as Mistress Anne, my father died in an accident when a horse pulling a farm cart was spooked and ran into him. On finding out that we had been thrown out of the room we had rented whilst father was alive, Lady Elizabeth allowed us to live in an old disused and tumble-down barn a couple of meadows over from the manor house. This was next to the dirt track which led into the village, which did make it easier for us to get into the village and for the villagers to visit us. It had been lived in before so a fireplace and chimney had been put into the centre, part of the roof had required sorting out as the rain came in and although it had two stone walls the others were wooden and they needed attention, but to us with nowhere else to go it was perfect, and Lady Elizabeth made no charge to us for living there saying the work which mother did for her was ample payment.

In time we patched up the roof and mended the walls, mother traded her skills for materials and labour and even furnished our home, in truth only a settle, a chair, stool, bench and a table. We didn't have beds but just slept on a thick wedge of straw. The fireplace had shelves and some nooks, where the stonework had fallen away, which came in useful for storing and drying herbs. There were always bunches of leaves tied to a length of string which ran the full width of the barn and our pots were kept on some metal hooks which were originally for tying straw to when the barn kept livestock. We did not have a cupboard, only an old bench on which stood our jug of water and the scarce possessions we had. The few clothes we had were kept in an alcove to the side of the fireplace and although they did smell of wood smoke they were always dry and warm. The barn had been made into a very acceptable home mother had said.

We were normally at the big house every day as mother helped with the housework, with the laundry on washing day and in her herbalist capacity which was greatly admired and, we were given to understand, far superior to any of her peers. Mother also made up the odd potion for the villagers and then there were her midwifery skills which were normally traded for anything we could use or sell.

We were permitted to eat with the servants when we were at the big house and as we were there most days, we lived much better than some of the poor creatures which periodically came to the big house begging because they were starving and dressed in rags. We were grateful to the Boleyn family and we were very aware that others did not fare as well as us.

At night, mother would sit with me and teach me about flowers and herbs and roots and what they would cure, how to dry them for when they were out of season, how to try different things and what to watch out for. She was aware that although her learning was extensive and based on what her mother had taught her, there was always more knowledge to be gained and so it was impressed

6

on me to grasp every bit of wisdom offered. I learnt everything from mother, I had a good memory and Mistress Mary did teach me a little about letters, when no one was around as it was not proper, so I did have a basic understanding although I could never read a book, but it did help me mark down recipes so I could understand them, especially useful when fathoming new potions.

I loved learning the remedies and one day whilst talking with mother I started to boast about how wonderful I would be and how everyone would come to me when I was grown, and how I would be the best with my mixtures. Mother firmly sat me down and looked intently at me. I wondered what I had done wrong. "Season, there are people who would look badly on us for what we do. You need to be careful and guard your tongue."

"Why mother, all we do is help people, and everyone likes us so what can be wrong with that?" I looked curiously at her. Mother took my hand in hers and with her other hand tucked a stray piece of hair back into my bonnet, she looked directly into my eyes and with kindness said,

"Some people pretend to like us because they are afraid of us or what they think we can do, we are needed, we provide something which cannot be afforded by ordinary people. Our neighbours in these villages have no money for apothecaries or physicians, they come to us because there is no one else and they can trade a service or food or anything else which they have. Trust no one my sweet little Season and keep a tie on that tongue".

"I don't understand mother, apart from not coming to us any more what could they do?" It still did not make any sense to me.

"We are called many things, wise women, sages, cunning women but some think of us as witches", "Witches" I said astonished, "but we don't weave spells or conjure devils or make magic, all our work is for the benefit of people"

"If proved to be a witch you could suffer all manner of tortures. You can be drowned on a ducking stool or burnt alive and innocent people have suffered these fates as well as some true witches. People like us who have an ability to ease pain and suffering can cause jealousy and envy within the community. I like to think that we just help when we can but you need to remember no one is a true friend and all could turn on you in a moment if the right temptation is offered."

"But Lady Elizabeth wouldn't, she's your friend" I implored,

"Lady Elizabeth has been very good to us and by her good grace we live as well as we do, but if she felt any of her family was in the slightest danger she would turn her back on us. This is not to say she is a terrible woman, it's to say she is a good mother who wishes to protect her family as well as she is able." This information came as a shock to me, before this I had thought that we were genuinely liked, but after this moment I looked at everyone in a slightly different way.

It was shortly after this conversation that I had cause to think over mother's words.

.

CHAPTER TWO

Next day we were required at the big house as it was laundry week. Which generally meant that the bed linen was being washed which was a huge job and everyone had a part to play. I was to wash the shifts which were worn under the top grand clothes, these shifts were so fine that they were nearly invisible but my small hands were thought not to be as rough as the housemaids, and I had proper soap to use. Mother was to help the cook as everyone else was busy.

I was coming out of the kitchen with bundles of shifts ready for washing outside when I bumped into the one of the housemaids, Nell, who was in turn hurrying into the kitchen to get buckets to fill from the stream. The shifts were piled up so high I couldn't see over the top of them and was peering around the side, Nell came up on my blind side and we met square on, resulting in both of us falling down. I got up and giggled and then caught sight of Nell's face, "You stupid girl, you could have really hurt me!" she shouted in my face although she was only a few inches away, I was stunned but before I could say anything she launched into a tirade my young ears had never heard before, "I'm not a favourite here, I doubt whether the Mistress even knows my name, all I hear is Agnes and Season talked about as if you are part of the family. Some of us have to work really hard all day every day and share a room with others, we don't get homes given to us. We don't get to pick and choose when we work and we don't get any gratitude for all that we do. You get to wash the shifts, I get to scrub the linen sheets and afterwards bleach them, my hands will be raw and bloody by the time I'm finished and I will ache from head to foot, but your hands will still be smooth, you will not be emptying the piss pots

11

and collecting water from the well after just a few hours sleep, or in the kitchen preparing food when your eyes are so heavy they hardly stay open!" Such fury from Nell with no warning, so quickly. I had never thought she could be so cruel. "Get out of my way, they will be calling for me" she said and with a last cold look, she put out her arm, pushed me aside and marched passed.

The rest of the day I kept out of the way but kept replaying Nell's words in my head. Later that night, exhausted, we had settled into our home for the evening and mother was brewing a base ready to add the key parts for a balm. "What are you mixing?" I asked peering into the pot,

"Lady Elizabeth has asked for something to help one of the housemaids, her hands always become raw and sore after washday and the skin cracks and bleeds."

"Is it Nell?" I asked already knowing the answer, so much for no one caring about her I thought.

"Umm, I have already made some up and given it to all who are helping but I need some more for Nell as hers needs to be a little more concentrated as she suffers so bad. Can you stir this Season as I need to chop this up?" said mother indicating a heap of leaves, I took the wooden spoon and stirred the mixture over the fire. "Don't let it bubble" called out mother. While I was stirring I looked into the pot and as I did so tears came to my eyes as I was so upset over what Nell had said to me, she was only a few years older than me, and I had thought of her kindly, if not a friend then someone just the same as me which is obviously not how she saw it, underneath she didn't like me and that hurt. I stirred and thought, and became angry and I visualised Nell washing the linen. I then pictured her getting into bed rubbing her aching back. I pictured her hands tender and sore. I remembered the nasty words and I concentrated on her throat and wished it as sore as her hands, so sore she couldn't speak, so sore she couldn't say another nasty word to me and while I was thinking this my tears fell into the pot and I stirred them in. I went into my own little world. I was startled as mother came and grabbed the pot from me, "Season what are you doing I told you to not let it bubble", mother admonished me. She took the pot from me using her skirts to hold the hot handle. "I think it will be alright" she said mostly to herself. "Season off to bed, you are too tired to do this, I shouldn't have asked you after such a long day" she said and gave me a quick kiss on the top of my head. I didn't answer just took myself off to my straw bed and covered myself with my blanket and brooded over Nell.

I was busy the next day collecting mint, lavender and roses for laying between the clean linen. Mother had had a message saying she had to go to the village as the blacksmith's wife had gone into labour. Lady Elizabeth said I could sleep in the kitchen overnight as there was no way of knowing how long the baby would take. I asked to go, as I knew I would have to learn on the birthing of babies but mother said I was too young, and it would come in time as women never stopped having babies. So regretfully I stayed in the kitchen at the big house.

Cook was a caring lady, never having any children of her own she had a bit of a soft spot for me so always saved me something nice to eat, this time it was cheese and not the stuff with mould on. Cook did like a bit of scandal and gossip, although most of what she told me was too adult for me and I didn't understand half of it, but I would just nod and grunt like I knew. So there I sat in a chair in a warm kitchen with cheese, just imagining if Nell could see this. I cuddled down next to the fire until mother came and fetched me just as it was getting light.

It was not until late the next day I heard that Nell had not been at her work that day. Mother had given her the balm for her hands and I had assumed that they were still sore and bleeding and that she was unable to grasp anything without leaving bloody hand prints. Cook had asked mother for her advice and I went with her up to the small attic bedroom which Nell shared with another maid. Nell laid on her pallet propped up with cushions and pillows. A thought did go through my mind that Lady Elizabeth supplied her servants with pallet beds and I had to sleep on a wedge of straw but when I saw Nell this thought faded immediately. Her hands although red were healing very nicely,

15

but her throat and her face was a mass of wheals and red marks. She was trying to swallow some ale that cook had given her but this was obviously difficult for her as she was choking and it was evident this was painful for her.

Mother sat beside her and took a good look at her. Rather than ask her to speak mother asked questions and Nell nodded or shook her head to indicate the answer. "Nell did this come on after you applied the balm?" Nell nodded. Mother looked at her hands, "Season, I thought it may be a skin reaction to the salve, my quantities may have been out and it was stronger that it should be but as you can see the skin on Nell's hands is healing nicely. Did your skin itch, on your face and neck before you applied it?" Nell shook her head, "Did you eat or drink anything different to normal?" Again Nell shook her head, "are there any of these marks elsewhere on your body?" Another shake of the head.

"What do you think it is mother?" I asked feeling really sorry for Nell, she did look awful.

"I've never had this type of reaction before, it's like

a poison but none of the ingredients are poison, you know that. I have another unguent which I can put on the sores and I will brew a tonic for Nell to drink which will bring down the soreness on the inside of her throat. Season, I want you to sit with her until I get back, I'll brew the tonic downstairs in the kitchen here, but you come running if Nell gets any worse."

Mother left and I sat at the bottom of the bed. Nell looked at me, "Season, I'm sorry for the other day" her throat was so sore she could hardly speak and she was trying to swallow after every other word, "I was very tired, I had been scolded by cook in front of everyone and I took it out on you." she was in a great deal of pain. I think she was about to attempt to say something more but I edged up the bed so I was sitting closer to her,
"I thank you Nell for saying that, don't speak any more, it's forgotten." I then thought she needed cheering so I said, "Do you want to hear some gossip whilst mother is out of the way?" Nell nodded and grinned and I regaled her with some tittle-tattle I had heard that mother would definitely

not approve of. Not that I am proud of it but although I said it was forgotten, it was much harder for me for be able to forgive, her words cut me deeply and I did brood over it for much longer than I should have. Nell carried those red marks for several days and struggled to speak and it was only when I realised that I could also have been more careful and felt genuinely sorry and did forgive, did her wounds heal. It was a coincidence that when I did feel clemency she got better.

.

CHAPTER THREE

Following tradition in wealthy households, Mistress Mary and Mistress Anne were sent off to further their social talents, learn courtly ways, and become an asset to the Boleyn family and hopefully secure themselves a good marriage. First Mary went to France to serve under Queen Claude and then a couple of years later Anne followed.

During the period the girls were away, I grew up. I acquired the midwifery skills, honed my abilities on cures. I learnt tolerance, discipline and how to listen and evaluate a situation, and these were the more useful skills and the most difficult to gain.

The hardest lesson I learnt was grief, my mother suffered a seizure and no amount of medicines I offered would help her. Lady Elizabeth even asked her own physician to examine mother but there was no great miracle and, whilst holding my hand, she breathed her last.

I stepped into mother's shoes. I had her knowledge and I had the knack of putting together new potions to help an ailment. I was frivolous, mother would not have been pleased, and I had managed to make a very lovely face water treatment which Lady Elizabeth tried, her husband commented how smooth her skin looked one day, Sir Thomas Boleyn was not one to give compliments and Lady Elizabeth was very enthusiastic and supportive of any future ventures in this area. I think this extra small offering secured my place within the Boleyn household and so I was not cast out of the barn when my mother died as I was as valuable as my mother had been.

As I grew older I was called upon to advise and administer cures. My reputation as someone who could heal was well known in the cluster of small villages surrounding Hever. I was constantly trying new things, but I always tested them out on myself first. Lady Elizabeth was very good at procuring me ingredients which I was not able to gather myself or that cost money which I never had. She gave me some cloves and I was permitted to have some salt and I mixed these with sage and made a paste which when rubbed on your teeth with coarse linen cleaned them quite nicely. I was told that the King could not stand for foul breath near him so this was an important part of the Boleyn's daily routine whilst at court. Although I had my share of successes, some of my new concoctions did not necessarily end with the result I would have wished, and sometimes I was poorly from my own hand.

I was afforded much more privilege and liberty than the other household staff at Hever and although I did not hold a high positon in terms of stature I was treated with respect by Lady Elizabeth and asked rather than ordered. This did not go unnoticed by the other members of the household and one or two of them were a little jealous of my relationship with Lady Elizabeth, especially Nell I think.

Mistress Mary returned to us in 1519 and went to court to proudly become a Lady-in-waiting to our good Queen Katherine. Less than a year later she married William Carey although they never seemed to spend much time together. Two years later Mistress Anne returned from France and came back for a short while to the house. Their lives were now so very different to mine and although I still spent a lot of time at the house, they did not come back very often preferring the excitement of court life and in Mistress Mary's case, her own household. On a rare occasion they were both at the house at the same time.

In the years away they had developed into young women. Mary had a soft beauty about her and was still very kind and gentle, although rumours ran rife that she was a little too kind and had shared more than smiles with various gentlemen whilst she was away. I once heard Sir Thomas and Lady Elizabeth's raised voices, the subject being Mary's reputation.

Anne, however, was very different, very striking, visually not as pretty or sweet as Mary, but she definitely eluded an air of superiority, french sophistication had rubbed off on her, she was haughty but very clever and knowledgeable about subjects which were usually confined to men and women would not be interested in. This endeared her to the males she was speaking to and she could converse cleverly. She could switch from being charming when the situation dictated to argumentative and sullen when attention was drawn away from her.

Standing next to them I was so painfully aware of my failings. Mary's golden hair, Anne's dark eyes, both girls blessed with an enviable figure, both highly educated, from a good family with wealth and it showed. I stood in my humble day dress, the hem torn from constantly going out into bushes and brambles sourcing ingredients, the ties on my bodice stretched as my amble frame was kept within. My hair a tangled mass of red curls with no neatness to it. My arms were covered in scratches and bruises, I never wore sleeves as they got in the way and the last pair I had I grew out of. I had just a coarse linen shift under my brown wool dress.

"Season, I hear you have made something for the complexion. Do let me try it, mother is very enamoured with it." Mary looked at me and gave me a gentle smile,

"Mistress Mary I will make some afresh for you in the morning" I said pleased,

"Why can't she have some now" said Anne looking me directly in the eyes, "I don't want to wait, I want to try it straight away. Mother's skin looks so young, so if it will work for her old skin, on mine I will be radiant!" Anne looked at me, more challenging me and at that moment I decided that Anne would have to wait considerably longer than it took to make up the mixture.

"Sorry, the preparation needs the freshest of ingredients gathered early morning and made whilst the day is at its coolest. I wake up at sunrise to gather all that is needed and prepare it, it then needs to rest before adding the final ingredient, the procedure cannot be rushed. You will be delivered some as soon as it is ready but it will be a while". I did already have some prepared but I was not going to admit that after Anne was so abrupt and mentally I worked out the order of delivery. Lady Elizabeth first, Mary second and much, much later will be Anne I thought. Anne grunted, sniffed and walked away with her nose in the air.

"I don't need it anyway." I heard her say as she flounced away.

"You'll get used to Anne, she's got a bit precocious since she's been in France. Used to getting her own way." said Mary looking embarrassed and obviously feeling she had to explain Anne's actions. I smiled at Mary. How could two sisters be so different?

.

CHAPTER FOUR

Mary's life moved on quickly, as a Lady-in-waiting to Queen Katherine she was as close to the Queen as you can get and she was also constantly in the King's presence and it seems that pretty Mary caught his eye. Although common knowledge at court, I was very shocked when I learnt that Mary had become the, "King's Mistress", however the Boleyn household regarded this as advancement and were proud of this achievement. I wondered what her husband William Carey thought of the matter.

The Boleyn household did well for Mary's

involvement with the King, although the one conversation I had with Mary showed she wasn't quite as happy as everyone else. Mary's husband had to keep his distance from her and she did miss him. I think she would have been quite happy to disappear and live quietly as an ordinary farmer's wife as she did not take as much pleasure from the jewels and fair clothes as her sister did, and she was always prepared to help others. Anne would never help anyone else unless she would benefit from it.

In time Anne also became a Lady-in-waiting to our beloved Queen Katherine although I think she relished this appointment more than her sister. Months would go by without either of them coming back to the house, there being much more exciting things to do at court. When the sisters were back there was always some drama usually centering or caused by Anne. I overheard Anne making terrible remarks about Mary's involvement with King Henry. Then Mary shouted back on one occasion, that, "It wasn't my choice. The King desires it and I could not refuse or the family would suffer because of it". Anne had replied that Mary should ask for more from the King as she was, "His whore!" Then she followed up the retort with, "You never got anything from King Francis either. Mistress of two Kings and not a penny to show for it. I would never let myself be treated in such a way. I will choose the man I want and they will pay handsomely for me. I will never be a slut like you, I will never be as stupid as you". I could hear Mary sobbing. It was shocking to hear, and I wished I had not heard the altercation, I felt uncomfortable and ashamed I had listened and was relieved they did not know I was near.

Anne was totally self-absorbed, she had ambition and the ruthlessness to get what she wanted. There was talk of a marriage with the Earl of Ormond but that never materialized, I know not why. I was never privy to such information and conversations would stop dead when I entered a room. I know Anne teased and simpered each time a possible beau was considered, and then she would say they were not good enough for her. After what I heard her say to Mistress Mary I knew that she would stop at nothing to achieve her dream of wealth, position and power.

Then Anne met Harry Percy and her guard came down. Anne did really care for this man, as much as I had seen her care for anyone. He was a good match for her, even by her own exacting standards. They were desperately in love with each other and that was evident to all who saw them together and it was lovely to see another side of Anne. On one occasion when Anne and Mary were home Anne was very excitable and talked about Harry Percy incessantly even to me, but this was when everyone else had tired of the subject. An agreement was made and both sets of parents were in favour and the arrangement was made to ask the King's blessing.

New gowns were ordered for the occasion, I benefitted too as the girls where in an exuberant mood and they looked out some old items for me. They said they would be dancing and having a good time, so I could put on something new and dance as well, the Boleyn's were putting on a little celebration for the estate workers in view of the impending wedding. I had the good fortune to be given an old pair of sleeves from Mistress Anne and a kirtle and some braiding from Mistress Mary, which was well needed as my own clothes were very threadbare. This didn't go un-noticed by Nell, but I do know that Mistress Mary did give her some braiding, an underskirt and a piece of lace, so she was not forgotten. Normally I didn't wear sleeves as they got in the way while I was preparing or preserving herbs. So sleeves were a luxury which were only worn on special occasions. The whole family was going to court to hear the King's blessing and approval, but this was just a trifle as Cardinal Wolsey had indicated it was as good as done. A high-spirited time was anticipated, the King did know how to banquet and keep his guests entertained. There was lots of chatter and general excitement. Plans being made about Harry Percy and Anne's future. The whole family was as happy as I had ever seen them.

I was expecting them to be at court for several months so I was surprised when, standing in the back hallway I saw Anne come through the door like a whirlwind, her face as black as thunder, her dark eyes red as if she had been crying . The rest of the family followed even Sir Thomas had come back. All looking distinctly displeased and serious.

I was bursting to know what had gone on but as just a servant I knew to keep my place. However, I was to find out shortly as a rumpus started. Lady Elizabeth was standing at Anne's door imploring her to open it. Anne was shouting that the King was, "An imbecile and an old fool who had forgotten what love was being married to a dried up old crone!" Then she said that, "He couldn't even manage it with the Queen, he needed mistresses like Bessie Blount and our Mary". Anne was talking with such disrespect about the King and Queen of England! When it was noticed I saw the commotion I was sent away from the house by Lady Elizabeth.

It was weeks before I was summoned back and that was by cook who needed something for a sniffle she had but I think really it was for a gossip. By this time they had all gone to court again but the atmosphere was still uneasy. Cook came and found me, "What a to-do that was!" she said, she looked about her to make sure no one else was within earshot, although everyone but me already knew. "The King denied the marriage",

"That much I had worked out for myself cook" I said with smile,

"It appears that the King has tired of the one Boleyn daughter and now wants to try the other." I was completely scandalised by what I had heard. My mind reverted back to Anne's conversation with Mary. The King would not find Anne as uncomplicated or easy going as Mary. "That's why the King said no the marriage, he wants a bit of her for himself. He doesn't want Mary anymore, she's old news. It does mean Mistress Mary can spend proper time with her husband now I suppose. Cook was looking at me and grinning, pleased with the matter of fact way this information had been delivered and the reaction she was getting from me which was utter disbelief. "Thank goodness we had our party on the night they left otherwise it would have all been cancelled now and all that food would have been wasted". Trust cook to be practical.

A couple of weeks later, I was preparing to make some pomanders which were needed to ward off the evils of nature, scent against the odours of everyday life and keep diseases at bay. I had large supplies of cinnamon, cloves, rose oil, rosemary and lavender and was grinding these up, ready to be mixed with beeswax. When blended together it becomes a malleable pulp which would then harden and go into the ornate pomander cages for the ladies to wear about their waists at court.

I was totally engrossed in my labours and was surprised when Anne with no introduction opened the door and strode straight in. Anne had never come to my home before so I knew instantly there was something of a secret nature she wanted to discuss but I was quite cross that she felt she could enter my home without calling out or knocking on the door.

She made no apology for her entrance, which was typical of her. It was obvious to me that she was embarrassed and she kept fumbling with her fingers and smoothing her gown with her hand. I had never seen Anne so perturbed. "Season I need you to make me a special tonic." she said looking out of the window and not straight at me, "As you know I was going to marry Harry Percy, as far as everyone was concerned it was going to happen and I now find myself in an awkward situation."

"Yes Mistress Anne" I replied although I had an inkling as to the direction this conversation was going, so I looked at her waiting and wanting this to be as uncomfortable for her as possible.

"I may possibly be with child" she said and then looked directly at me, "I had hoped to provide Harry Percy with a child quickly after my marriage to prove my worth to him." she said as if to justify her actions.

"What makes you think you may be with child, have you missed your courses?" I asked,

"Not really, well only by a few days at present, but I feel tired and I just don't feel quite myself" she picked at the imperfect extra nail she had on her little finger, which she always tried to cover. "The King has decided to favour me and my possibilities at court have improved, I am always involved in the dancing, the plays, I am sought out for conversation, my opinion is asked, poems have been written about me, I could make a much better marriage than Harry Percy, so you see I cannot have a child it would ruin everything for me. My mother married beneath her and I have no intention of doing the same." Same selfish Anne I thought to myself.

"Mistress Anne, I think it is too early to tell if you are with child, with all the events of late, your disappointment over your marriage, the whirlwind of your social activities could account for the tiredness, I think you need to wait a few more weeks until" Anne interrupted,

"I can't wait, I have to know and it can't happen, what can you give me to make my courses come?" Anne then suddenly lurched forward and grabbed me by the arm, digging her fingers in and upsetting the pestle which contained the contents for the pomanders, "Look at me" she said viciously, her black eyes boring into me "I can't have this ruin me, I was promised to Harry Percy and that makes us as good as wed, he can go off and live his life but I will be disgraced if this comes out! You will help me, you owe it to me," she thought a little and looked around my home then said, "You owe it to my mother as she has been extremely good to you." With that she released her grip but at the same time pushed me roughly to the ground.

Looking up at her I was quite calm in my response even though I was shaking with fury inside, "I have not the skill to rid you of the life you may have inside you or the inclination to do so. A life is sent by God and only he can take it from you. Any indiscretion you have brought to yourself is of your own making. If you have made a child enjoy it or give it to someone who will cherish it. You may find that it is the only time that God will bless you."

Anne's face was demented in anger, she was used to getting what she wanted. With sheer rage she picked up my stool and flung it against the fireplace, bringing down a layer of soot and shattering the leg of the stool in the process. I cowered back, covering my head with my arms and wondering what else she would do, bracing myself for the worst but Anne just turned and stomped out of the door slamming it with as much malice as she could muster. I took a deep breath trying to take in what had just happened, my heart was beating so hard I thought that all of Hever could hear it.

I was not called up to the house for some time after that incident and I was thankful as I did not wish to see Mistress Anne. I can only assume that Anne went back to court and the, "Awkward situation" of which she spoke was a false alarm as I heard nothing further. Months passed and I was pleased that Anne was away at court, it was so much nicer when she was away.

CHAPTER FIVE

The year of 1528 started normally and routinely but by the end of May a sickness called the "Sweating sickness" was sweeping London. Its actions were quick, a victim could be feeling a little unwell in the morning and by sunset God would have taken them. Generally in the country we did not see much of the diseases which affected the dense population of the city but in this case the sickness was relentless in the victims it was claiming all throughout the land. Things took a turn for the worse when Mistress Anne came back from court suffering from the sickness. She arrived home and was taken straight to her chamber. The King sent one of his own physicians to tend to her, although it may already be too late as within the space of a day she could be taken. Lady Elizabeth was obviously worried and the household was a flurry of sombre activity. Dr. Butts, the physician the King sent, was sending regular updates to the King via messengers. There is always one waiting to take news.

I was collecting roots from down by the stream, by the meadow furthest away from the main house. I was knee deep in the water with my skirts bundled up and tucked into themselves showing my legs over the knee and a voice calls out, "Mistress Season Cobb I presume?" I was lost in my own thoughts and the words surprised me. Looking up I see one of the messengers standing on the bank gazing at me in a bemused way with a smirk on his face. I hurriedly untucked my skirts allowing them to fall into the water and recovered myself,

"I am sir, what do you want from me?" The messenger was a tall fellow and of good physique. I could see the outline of muscles through the sleeves of his tunic, dark brown eyes and a generous smile.

"Lady Elizabeth Boleyn sent me to ask you to go to her. She was in a right old panic, everyone else is doing something and as the next update hasn't come through yet from old Butts I said I would come and find you. The name's Edward Short by the way, messenger, stableman and all round dogsbody and known as Ned by everyone!"

"I'll come straight away." My dress was now completely soaked at the bottom and weighing me down. I waded to the bank and the messenger approached the edge and held out his hand to help me, had I been on my own I would probably have climbed out on all fours but I felt a little decorum was needed as I was in company. The bank was slippery and the bottom of my skirt, which was heavy, wet and covered in mud adhered itself to my legs and as I attempted a little jump up to the bank my foot got caught in the hem of my dress and I slipped. I reached out in desperation and grabbed gratefully at the outreached hand, but in my panic I pulled the hand towards me, the result being I unbalanced the messenger and he lost his footing and slid down the muddy side bank and I launched headlong into him sending him on his back and myself sprawling on top of him. There was a period of absolute silence and then I felt the chest of the messenger heave. I have never been this close to a man before, not even when bestowing aid as normally I would tell the wife or mother what to do. I rolled off from him there is no other way to describe it. He was laughing! The shame of it all. My face burned with indignation and humiliation.

I scrambled up and grabbed the roots and other foliage I had been collecting and quickly put them in my basket. You can go "I said embarrassed.

"I cannot let a lady walk unaccompanied and I said I would take you back" he said, "although the Lady Elizabeth will be wondering what I have been doing to you, look at both of us!" We did look a state, and the infernal man started laughing again. "I don't normally make such an impression, but you are never going to forget me now Mistress Cobb, nor I you. I trust you are unharmed apart from your pride?

"I am quite well, thank you" I managed to say with as much dignity as I could manage. We walked across the meadow back to the house and although I wanted to stay mad I did find myself looking at him, and he caught me and smiled and it was a nice smile, not one that was making fun at me.

Lady Elizabeth was sitting on the seat underneath Anne's chamber window. Ned delivered me and then he left us. If Lady Elizabeth noticed anything about our clothing she did not speak of it. Her concerns lay elsewhere. As Ned left he whispered to me, "I will not forget the lady who threw herself at me" and I allowed myself to enjoy the moment.

Lady Elizabeth looked at me, "Season, is there anything you can do for Mistress Anne?"
"I'm sure Dr. Butts is more competent than I, and he has access to all manner of medicines I can only dream of. He will look after her".
"Season, I would appreciate anything you can do for her, and I will tell Dr. Butts you are to have permission to administer anything which may help, please Season." She looked fragile and suddenly a lot older than I had seen her before. More for feeling sorry for her than anything else I agreed to

look in on Anne and see if anything I could do would make her more comfortable.

Dr. Butts did not stay through the duration and when he was there he fell asleep in a side room, but I stayed awake all through the hours of Anne's illness, burning rosemary in the room to help cleanse the infection. She was ill, I did wonder whether it was put on or exaggerated in order to get the sympathy of the King, but when I was attending upon her I knew she really did have the sickness. I cooled her when she was hot, warmed her when she was cold, moistened her lips, cleaned her, administered my own compresses for aches and pains, tonics for headaches, but for the most part she was incoherent whilst the sickness rampaged through her. Dr. Butts did not do any more than I and he was worried for his own person, Anne is important to the King. There were regular updates to the King, although not much which could be said. In those prolonged hours caring for Anne I found myself thinking about Ned, how he smiled, how kind he looked, how his long eyelashes framed those gorgeous brown eyes and then reproving myself for being foolish.

The fever broke the very early hours of the morning. Anne seemed more rested, and my own exhaustion took over, I must have caught some sleep as I woke slumped over the coverlet. I was very stiff and uncomfortable and I stood up to stretch. I looked at Anne who was still sleeping but the beads of sweat had now gone and her general appearance had improved. I walked over to the window and moved the heavy drape to look out, I undid the window and leant out to breathe the fresh air. I did not advocate keeping rooms stuffy, however Dr. Butts had been very verbal on the subject so against my better judgement the room had remained closed in. It was still early, I could hear the kitchen maid. It was a still morning, no movement but I looked down and saw Ned with his knees drawn up to his chest on the seat under the window. His hose was still muddy and dirty. "Ned" I called out as softly as I could, I saw him stir and then look around before finally looking up. "I thought you had gone back to the court yesterday" I said.

"I was told to wait by Dr. Butts until I had proper definite news not just general stuff."

"But why are you out here, did they not find you lodging?"

"I bedded down in the stable with the horses, but they were also restless and I couldn't sleep. When dawn broke I decided to walk around, it's lovely here, and thought I'd rest on the seat. I did manage a couple of hours" Ned stretched and pummelled his thighs with his fists, his muscles were obviously stiff. "Any news?"

"I'll come down and bring you some ale, meet me around by the kitchen door" I closed the window.

Anne was still sleeping. I opened her door and called to Nell to watch over Anne,

"The pot will need emptying" I gestured to the piss pot in the corner of the room "Bring fresh water to Mistress Anne for washing and something for her to drink for when she wakes, I will be back shortly but in the meantime call me immediately if she stirs." Nell nodded.

I went through to the kitchen and was surprised at myself at how keen I was to see Ned. I got a jug of ale and some bread which had been newly baked and some cold meat and met Ned at the door. "Come and sit in the herb garden, there is an arbour." It was more a demand than a request but he walked behind me without question. "Before anything have something to eat and drink" I said pushing forward the ale and bread.

"How is the Mistress Anne?"

"Sleeping, but I think the fever has broken, she has stopped the sweat, still has a deathly pallor to the skin, but I wouldn't tell the King that if I was you. They will wake Dr. Butts and then you can have the official assessment and the exact words you can use when you tell the King." I wasn't sure that Ned was paying any attention to me as he was drinking his ale as if he had been out in the hot fields all day but he put down his tankard and wiped his mouth with the sleeve of his tunic.

"Thanks for the drink and thank you for giving the Mistress Anne back to the King, his behaviour would have been monstrous if anything had happened to her, he is devoted to her".

"Really?" I said and then covered my mouth with my hand, "Sorry I didn't mean that".

"Mistress Cobb I understand. The King who I greatly admire has fallen in love with Mistress Anne. Our Queen can do nothing but grin and bear it as she has done countless times before, but this time it is different, word has it that he wishes to put aside the Queen for her" again my hand went up to my mouth in shock.

"How do you know all this?" I said.

"Common knowledge at court, and I do hear quite a bit. I even have had conversations with the King himself!" said Ned with a satisfied grin on his face.

"Why would the King speak with you? I think you jest with me Master Short"

"Oh I'm not in the King's favoured circle, but I do look after his horses, and I am trusted to carry messages from the King to various ladies of the court. I was assigned to come down to Hever to carry news of Mistress Anne,"

"Are there other ladies that the King is interested in then?

"There are always ladies that the King is interested in. I took the blame for a dalliance he had at one time and he has never forgotten me because of it. The King is very discreet both for himself and the

47

ladies involved. He asked me at the time what favour I wished, and I declined saying that I wished only to serve him as best I could. Considering everyone is always asking favours of him I think he found it a refreshing change. I actually only wanted a quiet life but I have benefitted from it. I get to ride out on the horses from time to time, I take messages which earns me a coin or two on occasion so I'm happy."

"Does Mistress Anne know of these other ladies? What does she say? What does the Queen say?"

"Questions, questions Mistress Cobb" said Ned smiling,

"Oh sorry, but I don't hear much from court apart from when the Mistress Anne wants to boast about something, and I never hear anything about the King. What is he really like? "

"He's changed since meeting Mistress Anne, he's proper with Queen Katherine but the warmth has gone. He is cordial and polite and when the King and Queen are together it's like it used to be but the atmosphere changes when the Mistress Anne is in the room and that is now most of the time. I was about to ask further questions when we heard a voice calling for the messenger. "I'd better go Mistress Cobb," said Ned and stood up and gave me a little bow, "but I do hope that even though Mistress Anne is on the mend I will get to see you again" he said with a generous smile and in my heart I hoped that too.

Ned was given a message from Dr. Butts and hastened off back to the King. I did linger around hoping to see him again before he left but I was unlucky and I did feel a little disappointed. I looked in on Anne who had just woken and was feeling much better, Lady Elizabeth then excused me to go home and get some rest.

Although it was not wash day for another month I instructed that all Anne's bed linen be washed and it was hung out on the frames at the back of the house to dry. The chamber was to be scrubbed, anything which could be washed to be washed, fresh air allowed into the rooms and, until all had been washed and the surfaces dried, no fresh rushes to be laid. The housemaids were not happy with me and I did hear them complaining about me causing all the extra work however Lady Elizabeth obviously agreed with me as no official word of rebuke came my way concerning the added work which I was doling out.

When she was conscious we had to inform Anne that William Carey, her sister's husband had died from the sickness. Mary was distraught, and Anne did show some sympathy, a trait I would not necessarily associate with Anne. Clearly Anne had had some time to think about how close she had been to dying and the next conversation I had with her surprised and stunned me.

I found Anne sitting on the bench where her mother implored me to help her. "I have heard what you have done for me and the kindness and loyalty you have shown to me. Mother tells me you stayed with me the whole time. I wish," she hesitated whilst she thought of the exact words to say, "I hope that you accept my sincere thanks. My brother-in-law was not so fortunate, had he had you to look after him he may have survived. I do consider myself blessed that I had such good care, and on occasion

I have not treated you well and been unfair with you, when your wisdom proved more knowledgeable than mine. Thank you." I think she was referring to the incident many months before when she pushed me to the floor. Anne's face was showing an earnest quality which I had not seen before, and I did feel at this moment that what she was saying was heartfelt. I felt I may have been a little harsh with her so resolved to be more tolerant of her in future.

It had been a while since I'd talked to Ned and although I knew he probably hadn't given me a second thought now he was back at court, I found myself thinking about him a lot. I'd never had any attention from men, not attention which was wanted, a vulgar remark or two from men when they had had too many ales or invitations from men who were married and ought to know better, but Ned felt different and although he hadn't exactly given me any reason to expect anything further, something within me felt quite giddy when I thought of him.

CHAPTER SIX

When I was a child I discovered that chickens and fowl had forked bones which joined the neck to the breastbone. Mother pulled this bone out of a freshly cooked bird and told me to make a wish but not to tell anyone as it wouldn't come true. Mother and I closed our eyes and put our little fingers round the bone and wished and pulled and when it broke I had the larger part and won the wish. I secretly wished for a pocket to wear as I thought it was very grown up to have a pocket to put valuables in, even though I had nothing of value to put into it. When it didn't instantly appear I was disappointed and lost faith. A couple of weeks later

Lady Elizabeth was clearing out some of Mistress Mary's things and gave mother a petticoat and a pocket made from linen for me. I never told mother as I thought this might reverse the wish but ever since then I believed in the wishing bone but I knew it could not be hurried.

As a result of this each time I was able to get hold of one of these wishing bones I kept them. Very few of them I wished on, I was content to save up the wishes as in my mind the more unused wishbones I had the stronger it would make the wish when I made it.

One evening as I gazed into the night sky and the air was cooler than it had been all day, I sat down on the step in the doorway of my house and leant back, arching my back to stretch then pulling up my knees and rested my chin on them. Not in any way ladylike but comforting in a childlike way. I glimpsed a couple holding hands and running into the meadow, I could hear them laughing, I think I knew the girl, a marriage had been arranged for them. Would I ever be married? Mistress Mary was married and had two children by my age although now she was a widow. Deep in thought I was startled when an unexpected gust of wind knocked over my jar of wishing bones which was kept above the fireplace onto the earth floor Luckily the jar was still intact, had it fallen on the stone hearth it would have been different. I picked up the jar and sat back down again emptying out the wishbones. I counted seventeen and then I arranged twelve of them all touching each other in a circle on the floor and in the middle, with an absent mind, I drew a heart. I took up three of the wishbones and clasped them between both my hands and I wished for love. So concentrated was my efforts that when a neighbour called out, "Good Evening" to me from his horse I realised I had been sitting there for an age and the three wishbones in my hands were all crushed and broken, I buried all fifteen wishbones in the garden as they could not be wished upon again.

Days passed in normal repetitive chores. I returned home one afternoon, tired and drained as I had attended a long birth and found a visitor in court livery waiting at the door. At first I thought it was Ned as I all I saw was the livery, but my heart went from joy to disappointment within the moment. "Mistress Cobb?" the visitor asked, I inclined my head to acknowledge "I have this for you" and he handed over a large package and a letter.

"Please come in to refresh yourself and there's a water trough for your horse around the side." I gestured to the side of the house with my hand, my tiredness was momentarily forgotten. I put down the package and letter and served my guest a cup of ale, I wondered why Ned had not offered to bring it and I was saddened. I opened the package, I would have liked to appear nonchalant that I got packages everyday but I was too eager to see what it was and I undid the large green ribbon which held the contents inside. Nestling within was another layer of fine material in which was wrapped a pair of white sleeves, made beautifully in a fine brocade material with embroidered sprigs of sage also in white with a touch of green on them. They took my breath away and the material was scented so I was enveloped with a heavenly aroma. Who had sent me such a wonderful gift? I looked at the guest inquiringly and he pointed to the letter. I broke open the seal, I had never had a letter before and looked upon the words written but that is all I could do as my very limited knowledge of letters did not enable me to read the content. My guest seeing my difficulty stepped towards me and suggested,

"If I can be of any assistance to you Mistress?" and he gently took the letter from me.

"Most Gracious Lady" he read,

"I send this token in gratitude of the care taken of my most beloved Mistress Anne Boleyn.

Mistress Anne has told me of your ministrations and I am most thankful to you. I understand from the Mistress Anne that you do not have sleeves to wear so I hope this gift is welcome.

Henry Rex"

My jaw dropped open. King Henry, the actual King had written me a letter and sent me a present! He signed the letter, his actual writing was on the paper. Looking at the visitor, I must have looked a complete fool as I did not know what to say and my head did not quite take in what had just happened.

Calming myself I said, "Can you please read the letter again and will you run your finger along each word." I was curious to know what each word looked like written down. The guest smiled,

"Of course Mistress, and was there any reply?"

"No, yes I'm thrilled, I'm bursting with joy, thank the King, thank the King so much, this is a beautiful gift and I am honoured I could be of service" I must sound like a complete idiot to this man rambling on in such a fashion.

"Oh there is something else" said the guest and he held out another letter, this time with no seal and my name, which I could recognise on the outer part, two letters in one day, this was unbelievable. I took it from him, opened it and the only part of this one I could read was the name at the bottom which said "Ned". I looked at the guest trying to hide the obvious excitement on my face "Are you sure you wish me to read this one?" he asked, and no I wasn't sure but there was no way I was ever going to find out the contents so I nodded with more than a little enthusiasm.

"Dearest Mistress Cobb,

I hope this finds you well and I send good wishes to you. I find myself thinking of you and I would have liked to deliver the King's message myself, however his gracious highness had other plans for me, so my good friend Jasper was chosen.

I have business in the area of Hever to attend to on behalf of the King soon and wondered if I may call on you at that time?

Yours Ned Short

"Is there any answer to that one" said the guest whose name was apparently Jasper, I felt myself blush and thought for a moment,

"Tell Master Edward Short that I thank him for his good wishes and send my own and tell him I would be very pleased should he wish to visit me." Jasper dipped his head in a little bow and turned to leave when I said "Take care on your way home and remember to pass on my thanks to our blessed King for my wonderful sleeves and, my message to Ned"

"Thank you and you can trust me to deliver your messages just as they were spoken to me. I hope we will meet again" he replied with a hint of amusement on his face.

I was exhausted and fell into my bed but I did have little smile on my face. King Henry had written me a letter, he had sent me a gift, but more importantly Ned was coming to see me. Today had turned into a surprising day, a glorious, wonderful, delightful day.

I was not one for dreaming or pretending my life will ever change, I am content with what I have but fanciful thoughts entered my head and unpractical, emotional feelings dominated my hours for the first few days after Jasper came with the note from Ned. I found myself staring at the words written and I deluded myself that I was learning the letters, whereas I was really absorbed with the idea that Ned liked me and I really liked him.

Time passed very slowly and I had no idea when Ned would come to visit but I played out scenarios in my mind as to what would happen when we next met. I had a romantic inclination that I would be freshly washed, my hair smelling of the latest rose water I had concocted, wearing the sleeves the King had sent me and my best gown and I only had two to my name, going about my business, however the reality of the meeting was very different.

CHAPTER SEVEN

Over a month had passed and I had heard no word from Ned. There was a general un-wellness in the village, dizziness, vomiting, fainting and the like. It was not the sweating sickness but people were frightened and needed reassurance. There was not much that I could do apart from keeping them clean, making sure that they drank water from the well and rested as much as possible.

After a gruelling night I returned home mid-morning. I had planned to experiment with my ingredients and hopefully put together a remedy to help with the queasiness to do with this latest ague, but I felt sick and my head felt strange and I went to pour myself a cup of water. I reached up to get my cup which must have been the deciding element and with a ferociousness which still surprises me I vomited on the floor and all down the front of my gown. I then could not stop, I bent forward clutching at my stomach and another wave came over me. My head was spinning, and the taste in my mouth was vile, I need to cleanse my mouth with water, again as I reached up another spasm gripped me and then I remember falling, my head hitting the dirt floor.

I opened my eyes and just as quickly closed them again as the sun coming in through the window was blinding me. I put my hand up to my eyes and opened them again. I could see the outline of two figures. One of them approached, "Season, we were so worried." it was Nell! I pushed myself up on my elbow, I was at home, laying on new straw, and I was wearing only my shift. My hair felt wet to the touch. I grabbed at the cup of water offered, and it felt very good to wash away the terrible taste in my mouth. "Season, how are you feeling now?" Nell knelt beside me,

"I obviously got the sickness myself" I said with a weak smile at Nell.

"Yes you did, we had been expecting you at the house and when you didn't come I thought something was odd so I walked down"

I've been so awful to Nell in the past and now she was the one here, "When did you find me?" I asked.

"I walked down last night and when I got here you already had a visitor" said Nell and inclined her head to the other figure in the room. Puzzled I looked over and the visitor stepped into my vision, it was Ned!

"Ned what are you doing here?" I almost screamed at him as excitement and eagerness surged through me all at once.

"Season, what a shock you gave me," he said

"And what a shock you gave me" said Nell looking at Ned.

"I came as I said I would, but I had no way of letting you know and I was a little later in the day than I thought. I came to your house and the door was open, all I could see was a crumpled heap on the floor, and then I realised it was you!". I'm not sure that I appreciated being called a crumpled heap but I am sure that the description was accurate, Ned continued, " I turned you over and you looked very pale, and your clothes absolutely stank, there was sick and dirt in your lovely hair, and I did wonder if I'd already lost you before I'd even managed to get you." Not the scenario that I had pictured, but I focused on what he had just said, "My lovely hair" and he thought he'd, "Lost me before he'd got me!" I must still be feeling more unwell because I had a fluttery feeling. "Nell arrived just at that moment, just as I had my arm around you, luckily she could see exactly what had happened so there was no awkwardness. She's cleaned you up, washed you and she's washed your clothes. I went out and got new straw and have cleaned away as much of the foulness on the floor as I could and got a bucket of fresh water. Then we just stayed with you" Ned took my hand, "I just couldn't leave you" he added.

I did feel at bit shaken but after copious amounts of well water, I did feel much better, my spirits were lifted that Ned and Nell stayed with me. I am ashamed to say that when I felt a little better I wished Nell would go back to the house so that I could be alone with Ned, but she stayed and looked after me. I made mental note to be a lot more forgiving of Nell as obviously she had a heart of gold and perhaps I had been the one at fault in our past misgivings. As Nell and Ned had been up all night with me, Nell sat down on the settle, her intention to tend to the fire, but tiredness overtook her and her head nodded onto her chest and she dozed. "I think you should now have a rest Ned, I am so much better now,"

"Season just before I do. I have to go back to court tomorrow and I don't know when I will next be able to see you again. If you are willing I will take every opportunity to deliver messages and do the King's bidding if it means seeing you. I may be able to send a message through sometimes but I can't promise, but I would like to know if it would be well received".

"Ned anytime you have I would love to spend it with you. I would look forward to it. Although it will be difficult I will always be here" I said and meant it. I could see Ned was really tired, "Lay down a while and rest Ned as you have a long journey ahead tomorrow". Ned very slowly bent his head towards me and gave me the faintest glancing kiss on the lips.

Ned was true to his word. If there was a chance to get to see me he did or send me a message but sometimes it was months before I had any word from him. This arrangement had been going on for more than a year and Ned's visits sometimes only lasted a couple of hours and if totalled up together we had probably spent only 4 whole days together and that was normally in someone else's presence. One morning I was tending to my chickens and I heard the familiar pounding of a horse's hooves and was thrilled to see Ned dismount. He threw the reigns of his horse down and ran over to me sweeping me up and swinging me round. He squeezed me so tightly I thought I would never breathe again and when he finally put me back on my feet he landed a heavy kiss. I was amazed, never had Ned expressed such emotion before. "Season it's been so long since I saw you, over 4 months, I was beginning to wonder if ever I would see you again. There has been no cause for anyone to come out this way so I couldn't even get a message to you. I have been turning myself inside out wondering whether another has stolen you away from me." He took my hand and bustled me into my house.

"Ned there is no one else for me," I said to reassure him, "How long do we have together this time?" Ned grinned.

"We have a whole week, for 7 days I can be with you, I can take you out on my horse, we can eat together, we can walk together, talk, laugh. I don't want you out of my sight".

"A whole week!" I exclaimed.

"And don't worry I have booked myself in at the local Inn so there is no improperness" I blushed awkwardly. At no time had Ned ever acted improperly, but there was a feeling inside me that half wished that he would.

It was truly a wonderful time for us. I still had my duties to attend to but rushed to get through them so I could spend as much time with Ned. One evening we were sitting in my house, the fire roaring and we had just finished a rabbit stew. I sat on the chair, Ned sat on the settle and we were very relaxed and easy with each other. Ned said, "A lady was alighting from a carriage the other day, I was holding the door open for her and Jasper was trying to quieten the horses, they were disturbed by a rat that was running across the courtyard. One of the horses was spooked and jolted forward, moving the carriage and the lady missed her footing and caught her shoe in the hem of her dress."

"Was she alright?" I said moving from the chair and sitting beside Ned on the settle,

"She stumbled and I caught her but not before she tore the hem of her gown and ripped the front of her bodice on the latch of the carriage door".

"Oh goodness. Was she angry?"

"No she took it in good part, she said she didn't like the rats any more than the horses did! But the rip in her bodice tore the stitching and spilled large teardrop pearls all over the ground. I picked them up, and gave them back to her and she thanked me."

"I should think so too, if you hadn't caught her she may have hurt herself".

"I think Jasper was worried that she may complain, but she was a very nice lady, I have seen her before". Ned then edged even closer to me on the settle, he took both my hands in just one of his, "The nice lady handed me back the largest pearl which dropped on the floor and told me I should keep it with her thanks. I said it wasn't proper to keep it but then she said it also wasn't proper for her to fall into a man's arms who is not her husband and then she laughed."

"It seems to be a habit of yours to have women fall into your lap" I said remembering our first meeting with a grin. "Is it worth a lot of money" I asked and then thought it was not a question I should have asked.

"I think it is" said Ned, and he then reached into his tunic and pulled out a leather pouch. As he reached inside at the same time said, "I asked the saddler to fashion me a length of leather and I had the pearl put onto it with a metal ring and now it is for you." The pearl slid out of the pouch attached to a leather thong. Ned secured it around my neck and my fingers went up to the pearl which felt smooth and cool against my skin.

"Ned it's gorgeous" I said admiring its lustre. I'd never had something as lovely as this apart from my sleeves.

"It looks beautiful on you, and I hope when we are parted it will remind you of me".

"Ned I never stop thinking about you, and I'll never take it off". Ned traced around the outline of the pearl on the top of my chest where it lay. He looked at me and then very careful ran his finger along the neckline of my gown which was much lower than where the pearl hung around my neck. I felt myself quiver inside, he leant into kiss me and moved the top of my gown so it felt over one of my shoulders and then he kissed the naked flesh. Even with my limited knowledge of love I knew where this was all going and if I was to stop this I would have to say now.

Ned didn't go back to the Inn. We stayed together all night.

.

CHAPTER EIGHT

That week together was something I thought about often and longed to happen again. I stroked the pearl around my neck and I wouldn't take it off at all, I told everyone about it and showed it off at every opportunity. I happened to be at the big house tending the herb garden when the Mistress Anne came back. It was like she purposely looked for me. After a couple of comments made about court which really didn't interest me, the real reason Mistress Anne was so keen to talk to me became apparent. "I understand you have being seeing Edward Short of the King's stables Season" Anne said smirking, if Anne was asking about Ned I felt sure she had something nasty she was going to say, so I didn't answer which aggravated her, "Edward is a lovely fellow, everyone likes him, so kind and gentle and funny and" what was she after I wondered,

"Yes he is all those things Mistress Anne",

"And handsome I was going to say" said Anne with what only be described as a sneer on her face. "Obviously he's only handsome in a servant kind of way not like our King who outshines everyone with his looks". If she was trying to annoy me I was not going to let it show but I did have a couple of barbs I could turn back at her,

"Do you think our King is as handsome as Harry Percy Mistress Anne?" I enquired spitefully, Anne flashed a poisonous look but I carried on, "All the handsome ones seem to be married don't they? Harry Percy couldn't live without you but he married Mary Talbot and of course the King is very firmly married to our wonderful Queen Katherine". I carried on weeding the herb garden but I was inwardly congratulating myself on getting one over on Anne, however, perhaps I shouldn't have been so vicious as then the purpose of her chatter became clear.

"Yes, I did think my future was with Harry Percy, but after I decided not to marry him" that was a blatant lie the King didn't give his permission but she continued, "he went off and married some harpy. Men cannot be trusted, take your Ned for example and he always seems so nice." she emphasised the word nice, "but he seems to have another maid in his life at the moment, a laundry maid for heaven's sake, mind you he doesn't set his sights too high does he if he's been interested in you? I saw him kiss her and embrace her and they looked very comfortable together. Ask him about it, he can't deny it, he knows I saw them together, and it's not the first time either and she's not the first maid either, talk is most of the females at court have had an encounter with Edward Short." After delivering this piece of evil gossip Anne waited for a reaction, and she got it. I threw down my weeding tool narrowly missing her and stood squaring up to her with my hands on my hips.

"Ned wouldn't do that to me, he gave he this" I pushed the pearl in front of Anne's face.

"Ah yes the infamous pearl, I think you wish to

mimic me Season, as you know I wear my B necklace frequently and that has three large pearls which hang from it. Ned did his best, however how many more maids has he given a trinket to just to secure a place in their bed". The anger and fury which exploded within me made me burst into uncontrollable tears and Anne loved it which made it even worse. Anne took so much pleasure in my shock and grief and while I ran past her she threw back her head mocking and laughing at me.

I so wanted to talk to Ned, I so wanted him to tell me none of it was true, because it wasn't, it couldn't be, what we have together it was just for us. Anne was just jealous. Then a creeping doubt entered my mind, yes Anne was vindictive and nasty but Ned would know that she would tell me that she had seen him. I had no way of getting a message to him and I had to wait until he either came to see me or send a message which I could reply to.

A very long seven weeks passed before I got my chance to speak to Ned. In that time I tormented myself, did he have other women whilst at court?

He must have, such prettiness against drab me there would be no comparison. Why then did he keep coming back to visit me for it was a long way on horseback? My mind turned it this way and that but I never could settle on a satisfactory answer.

I collected myself, I would not shout like a mad woman. Ned would have an explanation, it was all a misunderstanding. This is what I told myself and then that day Ned walked in the door and strode over to me ready to plant a kiss. I turned my head from him. "So what have I done to anger you Season? I have not seen you for nearly two months or is that the reason?" Ned said in a teasing tone.

"I have had word that you are keeping the company of another whilst you are at court." I said with a lot more composure than I felt, "What have you to say for yourself" I felt my voice waiver.

"It is nonsense Season, there is only you. Each time we part I long for the next time I can get to see you. I am not interested in anyone apart from you, who is filling your head with this?"

"A person with nothing to gain from it" I said but I

knew that if Anne knew we were having this conversation she would be delighted she had upset me again and that would be her gain. "You were seen in the company of a laundry maid who you embraced and kissed. That is not nothing Ned, or do you do this commonplace so one particular time does not stand out!" my voice had now risen, the anger creeping in.

"Really Season, tittle tattle from someone with nothing better to do. I thought better of you. Now come sit on my knee and let us talk about other things, I've been longing to see you". Ned sat down on the chair and patted his knee, just like he was ordering a lap dog to come to him. I am no lap dog and that action promoted an outburst which flowed from me. Even if I had tried I could not still that fire that burned within.

"No Ned, I will not be treated like an ale house whore, ready for you to pick up when you feel the need. As far as I know you could be in a different village every week doing the King's business, with a maid in each of them. Was it my turn today? I think I am due some kind of explanation and then you can be on your way." by this point I was screaming like a banshee at him, my exasperation and rage boiled through. It was then Ned got up from the chair, his face showed an expression I had never seen before, a combination of disappointment and anger. He drew a deep breath and looked at me and said,

"You are not the only woman I have ever known Season! I have loved before and I do not mean just in the physical way. I have truly loved, with all the passion, commitment and frustrations, with the compromises and heartache which comes from living for someone. I have known the feeling when you cannot think about anything else when you feel full to bursting and excited at seeing them to the exclusion of all other things".

"So who is this woman Ned, have you been biding your time with me until you can be with her again?" Hurt burned within me and my eyes started to sting with tears although Ned could not see them as he had turned his back on me.

"Season this wonderful woman of whom I speak was my wife". Ned said with a restrained dignity. "Was my wife", was all I heard. Ned, whose expression was contorted with a mixture of grief and wraith turned around to face me.

"My beautiful wife, my beautiful Eliza died 2 days after giving birth to our son. Our son died 2 days after that. In the space of a week I went from expectant father and loving husband to father, widow and then burying the two most important people in the world to me".

Deflated and guilty I stepped forward to Ned, but he walked away. "After that I lived my life without care or respect for others, if I love something it can be taken so easily away, so I said I would never allow myself to love again. I used women to my own gratification and cared not for them. I admit to that.

Flora is my wife's sister and she lived with us, although young herself she brought me through it, and it must have been rough for her for I was not good to her. Flora reminded me that the person Eliza loved and married had disappeared and the ogre left behind made a mockery of the love we had had together. I have love for Flora but as the good caring person she is, as Eliza's sister she is my sister too and yes I do kiss her each time I say goodbye to her and we do embrace and hug each other, as I know she too could easily be taken from me and it may look like something else to busy bodies who wish to look on but I make no apology for it."

"Ned how can I say how sorry I am" he cut me off before I could say more,

"You can't. You cannot possibly know what it is like. For the first time since Eliza I fell in love again, and I didn't realise it, Flora could see it and she convinced me that the guilt I felt over betraying Eliza was natural but that Eliza would want me to live on and love again. I was willing to take the chance with you" .

"Ned" I reached forward to him but he turned away. "I can't talk to you at the moment Season, leave me alone" he said and moved away from me. I watched as he walked out of the door, he didn't hesitate to leave me, he didn't even look back at me. Have I just lost the most important part of me, from being jealous and stupid? My insides churned and I felt sick. Could Ned forgive me, would he want to? I wish I could take it all back. Anne, it's her fault, she's just out to make trouble. I hate that woman.

That night I thought about our argument, and

wished I had been more patient and allowed Ned to explain properly. No amount of wishing on the bones would be able to clear the hurt away for either of us. Ned left that night without another word and I kept hoping he would send a message, or come to see me but weeks turned into months and I had to admit that any hope of us being together was now gone and it was I that was at fault, for believing Anne and not trusting Ned.

.

CHAPTER NINE

December 1529 I had a visitor. Jasper turned up on my doorstep. It had been ten months since I'd last seen Ned, there had been no message or visit from him and I knew that my jealousy had driven him away and I blamed Mistress Anne for it.

"Mistress Cobb do you remember me?" he said,
"Of course I remember you Jasper. Is everything all right? Is Ned all right?"
"That's why I am here. No he's not!. He changes between being melancholy and then abundant exuberance. It is hard to keep up with him. But the reason is you".

"The last time we saw each other it was not good. I don't know how much he's told you Jasper".

"He's not said much, and you obviously had a falling out, and it must have been a big one as he said you told him to leave which he did but wishes he hadn't. He knows you don't want to see him again. Did he do something really bad? If he did it's really out of character for him. He misses you so badly, each time he got the chance to see you he was so excited. Now he gets on with his work and makes every effort in front of the court being overtly too cheerful and happy but then he sits in an ale house all night and is really miserable."

I bowed my head, feeling embarrassed, Ned had not told Jasper the reason for the argument which I understood as being so painful for him. "What can I do Jasper? Will you take a message?"

"I think more decisive action is called for Season. That is if you really do want him back. Do you?" Jasper looked at me.

"What do you have in mind" I said.

A couple of hours later on was on horseback with a

bundle of provisions riding with Jasper to London and the court. I hastily made plans for who would feed my animals for the time I was away, and for which, heaven bless her, Nell stepped in again. Originally Jasper had been sent down to collect a horse and he had made a slight detour in order to see me, so we both rode his horse and the other horse trotted behind tethered by rope. I wasn't sure what I was going to say but the closer I got to London the more anxious I was to see Ned and the more nervous. I chatted with Jasper about nothing in particular during those long hours. We took a break to stretch our legs when we came by water, I suspect a break for me as I was unaccustomed to horse riding and was very stiff. Sitting with our backs against a tree having a chunk of bread and some cheese whilst the horses meandered, drinking water from the brook, I said to Jasper, "Did you know Eliza, Jasper?"

"Was that what it was all about?" he said,

"In part" I answered,

"I didn't actually know her but I did know about her. It was just after she died that I came to work alongside Ned and obviously he was full of sorrow.

83

Flora, Eliza's sister cared for him and put up with a lot from him. There's an understanding between them, as close as you can get, but don't get that confused with what he feels for you. Took him ages before he could bring himself to say Eliza's name and the baby, well they had looked forward to that so much, and he lost them both, poor bugger."

As a midwife on occasion I had to deal with the grief of a mother when the baby was born dead, and heart wrenching though it is I had never really understood that pain. The situation, the practicalities yes, but not the pain, it was not something I ever wished to experience. Just when I thought there was nothing left to learn I find another part of life of which I have no personal insight, just like my mother used to say, there is always something else to learn.

We travelled on and the fields became villages and then towns and then to the outskirts of London. This was new to me, so loud, so hurried, and so dirty and it stank so badly. The river that ran through London, Jasper told me, sometimes got so cold that it froze over and skaters danced on it but it was vile, a murky green and brown water with curious mounds of debris in it which floated around like little islands, one mound I thought was black was actually dozens of rats feeding on something indescribable, why anyone would want to dance on it was beyond me. I had never seen so many people all jostling each other and shouting over each other. There were tradesmen and street sellers all hawking their wares. Pies on trays being paraded under the noses of potential buyers whilst poor creatures who had not eaten for days looked on. Well-dressed people who held nosegays to their faces and looked on with distain at individuals who begged openly for anything which could be spared. In my village we all helped each other I wasn't used to seeing this and I found it exciting but also very sad.

The last part of the journey came to a conclusion when Jasper asked me to dismount outside of a very grand stone building. "Is this the court?" I said excitedly,

"No Season, this is just the stables. There is a

stone mounting block over there go and sit awhile while I sort out the horses and then I will be with you". I think Jasper was amused by my naivety but he kept his composure. I felt a bit stupid, the only fancy house I had ever seen was Hever and this was a huge building with a cobblestone courtyard and lots of pages dressed in livery, all craning their necks to take a look at a very poorly dressed country peasant. I couldn't believe this was just the stables. Then Jasper appeared,

"Where are we going?" I said as I fell into step beside him.

"You are now going to meet Flora, Ned's sister-in-law". I didn't know if I was ready to meet her quite yet, I was hoping to see Ned, although I had no idea what I was going to say to him. "Flora knew I was going to try and bring you back with me, so she will be pleased, but Ned doesn't know anything because we weren't sure how you really felt about him and we didn't want to make it worse". We walked away from the clean stable courtyard, through the filth of the street, which I picked my way through. A short walk, thank goodness and I was taken to a slim door which if you didn't know was there you would have missed, this was next to a dressmakers. Jasper opened the door and shouted up the wooden stairs. "Hello there, I'm back and just look what I've got!" A head covered by a white bonnet poked around the top of the stairs.

"Jasper" was all it said. Advancing up the stairs behind Jasper I felt my stomach turn a somersault, I was so nervous. I walked into a room, a large window filled the room with sunshine and I could see all the dust glimmering in the ray of light coming through. There was a table with some sewing placed on it. A fireplace with a pot dangling over the fire. A doorway off to another room. A settle, chairs, a rug a cupboard and a chest. More or less what I had at home but this was of better quality. In the middle of the room standing so the light fell upon her was a small girl who didn't look above 16 years old. She clasped her hands in front of her like she was being presented to royalty.

"Flora this is Season Cobb" said Jasper. Without any warning the girl lunged forward and flung her arms around my neck,

"I'm so pleased to meet you Season, Ned talked

about you non-stop and you are just as he described". I couldn't answer that one because Ned had never told me anything of her so I hugged her gently. "Come, sit, and let me take your cloak. Jasper get Season a drink" Flora pointed to a pitcher on the top of the cupboard.

"Here you are," Jasper handed me a drink, "I must go as I have duties to perform but I will be back later" Jasper winked at Flora who giggled. Left alone with someone I'd never met was daunting but Flora filled any embarrassing silences with a constant gabble of dialogue.

"Ned will be back soon and I need to get some supper for him, will you help?" Chores are a great leveller when it comes to making friends and chatterbox Flora was absolutely lovely. Jasper came back after his work and we sat chopping and peeling and chattering and then Jasper let out a tremendous loud bout of wind. Flora looked at me and then Jasper who said,

"Oh sorry was that me" and we all fell into uncontrollable laugher. So much was the hilarity that we didn't notice when Ned came into the room. The room fell silent. Jasper and Flora looked at each other. Ned looked from one to another. No one said anything. My throat felt like it had a large lump in it. I took a small step forward and then I rushed as quickly as I could and threw my arms around Ned and to my relief his arms encircled me and he buried his head in my neck. "I'm so sorry my darling Season" he said over and over again, whilst I uttered apologies and my regret. Not that I noticed at the time but Flora and Jasper left the room and left us alone together for the first time in over ten months.

.

CHAPTER TEN

We had supper all four of us and then I went for a walk with Ned. We talked for hours, we said sorry, we hugged and kissed and we cleared up the ill feeling. Understanding counts for a lot after an argument. It all felt so unnecessary the angst we had put each other through. Ned relinquished his bed for me and slept in the main room, it felt like we were only just meeting again. When I woke the next day, Flora was already working in the laundry. She started early at about five in the morning, Jasper lived in his own place and Ned was nowhere to be seen. I washed my face from the pitcher of water in the corner of Ned's bedchamber, tidied the bed, whatever had he thought of my bed on straw when he had a proper pallet bed. I took the broom which was in the hallway between the main room and the bedchambers and started sweeping when I heard Ned whistling and coming up the stairs. "Where is my sweet little Season?" he called. I jumped out in front of him with a grin on my face hoping to make him jump, honestly we were like children!

"I have brought us a feast. I have fresh milk, well sort of, not as fresh as you are used to, eggs, bread which has just been baked so won't pull your teeth out" he put down the jug of milk and eggs which were in a cloth and the bread tumbled from his arms and I only just caught it. "I have something to ask you. I wished I'd asked a long time ago and I thought I'd lost my chance. I am not going to miss another opportunity. He dropped to his knees. Season marry me, please marry me, will you?"

Two days ago I was at home, miserable, lonely and now the man I had pined over was looking up at me and was asking me to be his wife. There was no other answer, "Yes, yes, yes Ned!"

I was amazed at how quickly things got organised. Ned got us a date at the church. Flora worked in the laundry but also did some sewing for the dressmakers downstairs, so was able to procure me an old green wool gown which had seen better days, but in her expert hands it was patched, braided and given another life. In my provisions when I left Hever I had strangely packed the sleeves the King gave me, probably because they, apart from my pearl necklace, were the most precious things I owned. So I stood in a green gown, with an underskirt of cream with my sage embroidered sleeves. My slippers were borrowed from Flora, the only thing she could lend me as I am far bigger than she in every other way. My hair was fragranced and was arranged in such a fashion as felt most peculiar and a coronet of ivy, mistletoe and dog rose laid on my hair. I carried a posy of ivy and dog rose with sprigs of myrtle. My pearl was at my neck and my darling Ned was on my arm. This felt right. Flora asked if I would be upset if the wedding ring could be Eliza's. She said it would feel like Eliza was still with us all and although a strange request as had Eliza lived I wouldn't be here at all, it was comforting that I was trusted by her and I had no problem with it, I felt it would be an honour to wear it. Ned was touched by this gesture.

The first day of 1530 we were married with Flora and Jasper as witnesses. Everyone was rejoicing and out on the streets celebrating the New Year and it felt as if they were all celebrating and happy for us.

As wonderful as my life had just become. All too soon the practical side kicked in. After many conversations most of them filled with tears, we settled on what we thought was a situation which would suit us all. Ned could tell I would not be happy with living in London, I would miss the countryside and the quiet, and my animals and I know my place was with Ned and I was happy to give it up, but he wanted me to be happy too. He had saved some money but not enough, his plan was to save enough for him to leave the court and get a smallholding in the countryside. He thought he needed another year of savings so he would continue to work at court. I would go back to Hever and carry on as before and whenever Ned could get away he would. It would be a marriage with much separation but we felt it would work. Ned also felt he couldn't leave Flora as she wouldn't be able to manage on her own. So with a heavy heart just twelve days after I arrived in London I packed up and Ned took me back to Hever. When we got to the barn it was late, Ned stayed with me for that night and then left early in the morning for the long journey back. I waved at him until he was but a dot in the distance, tears spilling from my eyes.

CHAPTER ELEVEN

"When I said I would feed your animals, I thought it would just be for a day or two, not nearly two weeks" said Nell, "I'm worn out with work at the house then trudging down here, and they have been missing you up there, I said you were ill but they were starting to get suspicious". I thought she was angry but when I saw her face I could tell she was jesting.

"Nell I'm married!" I said thrusting out my hand for her to admire the ring.

"Married! Season how wonderful, Where is Ned?" she asked. I explained the situation and although she agreed it wasn't ideal she could see the benefit in it. I wasn't ashamed of being married I was very proud but I asked Nell to keep it secret, my business was nothing to do with anyone else and if cook got to know everyone would know and I didn't want Anne to find out. Cook however had her mind on other subjects and was still revelling in the news that Sir Thomas Boleyn had been created an Earl in December and was now a Lord. The whole family were very pleased at his advancement. One daughter in particular had boasted incessantly that it was due to her influence that he had a new title.

Now married to Ned I missed him so much, should I have stayed in London? He did get down to see me but there were long separations in between. Each time Ned came to see me he would bring any savings he had and I would sew them into the hem of the dress I had for my wedding to keep them safe ready for our new life together.

Six months passed and Nell married a huge hulk of a man, an estate labourer called John Todd but known as Toddy to everyone. Almost as soon as she was married she was pregnant and I was privileged to be there and deliver Nell of a son just over 9 months later. A large baby, even though they called him Little John and as a midwife I wondered how a frame of Nell's' could push such a huge child into the world. Wrapping him up and handing him to Toddy, that big man looked so strange holding a baby but tears of joy rolled down his face and the grin could have lit up the sky.

Ten months later I was back in the same place delivering another of Nell's sons. They were so very happy together and they had so little in material possessions, but love absolutely poured from them and I realised what I was missing out on. "I think I made a mistake" I said to Nell as I was helping her to get up after the second birth.

"With what?" she said

"With Ned", A shocked look crossed Nell's face, "No not that" I said to calm her, "I mean I should be in London with him and not here. You have a lovely husband and two fine sons to show for your marriage and I have still to experience baby pains even though I have been around them for as long as I can remember." Nell looked at me, "You must do whatever feels right for you, there's no right or wrong. If life goes wrong keep on at it and turn it around. Sometimes you have to make a wrong decision in order to recognise the right ones". Nell prepared herself to suckle her new-born, when did she get so wise?

"I'm worried about living in London, but I so miss Ned. It was only supposed to be for a year or so and it's much longer than that now, and I want what you've got Nell, I admit I am jealous of you but I wouldn't take anything from you I just wish I could have some of it."

"Oh Season I was so, so jealous of you when we worked at the house. You had freedom and were clever and people liked you and I wanted what you had." Nell smiled. How silly we both were when we were young and what time we wasted from being resentful when we could have been friends I thought. "I think you already know what to do" said Nell,

"Oh Nell", I hugged her even though she was suckling the babe.

Unable to contact him I waited until the next time

Ned was back. I told him I was returning with him for good. His face illuminated with pleasure. "I so wanted you to say that but I didn't want you to feel you had to. I had under estimated how long it would take me to save enough money for us, but I will make you happy my darling".

In the end I couldn't return with Ned immediately but two weeks later Ned sent Jasper and a cart to collect everything I owned. I had hoped I would travel with Ned but he had been sent on an errand for the King and Ned couldn't say "No" to King Henry. I had sold my animals apart from the chickens, one of which I killed and cooked for meat to eat on the journey, the others were in a cage, I thought I could trade them for extra money when in London. I packed all my ingredients, I had filled my days with collecting as many as I could and drying them as I didn't know what I would have access to in London.

The day I said goodbye to Nell, made me wonder if I was doing the right thing. We were both in tears and not much needed to be said. I knew I probably wouldn't see her again as it was unlikely I would return to Hever. We all hugged, Nell, Toddy, Little John and the new baby Arthur and me. I stepped up onto the cart, and was surprised to see that alongside Nell and her family, cook from the house, and several of the villagers had heard I was leaving. Cook gave me a cloth with some provisions within, bless her, a villager gave me a blanket she had stitched which was a thank you for the 9 children I had helped her deliver. Some people had even worked together to make me a new cloak to wear and I felt very tearful as I waved and they waved as the cart rolled away from my life at Hever. Jasper kept quiet until the people dispersed and we were on our own going to London to my Ned and a proper life as Mrs. Edward Short.

Surprises, such surprises. Jasper had kept the secrets. I'd only ever gone to London once when I got married so I didn't remember where Ned and Flora lived in relation to the city, but I was sure that Jasper went a different way. The house he drew up against was not the one I stayed in before, but he got down and waited politely to assist me in my dismount. Ned appeared in front of a tall skinny house which looked as if it would topple forward from the weight of the overhang of the upper storey. "Welcome wonderful wife, to your new home" he said with a grin and swept an overelaborate mock bow to me. I was a bit bewildered which obviously showed, looking round myself in puzzlement. Then the door to this skinny house opened and Flora appeared,

"Oh Ned, you're wicked" she said, "Kiss your wife and explain, and bring her inside" she said laughing. Ned put his arms around me and held me close and after all those hours on the road, the tiredness, the worrying and apprehension, I burst into tears and held him to me. This seemed to be a signal for Flora and Jasper to leave. When I had recovered myself a little Ned walked me in the door of this funny little house.

"I thought as you were giving up your life in the country, I could make things a little more comfortable for you here. I managed to find this place to rent which is big enough for us and Flora and it has a little courtyard out the back which is shared with two other houses but it is somewhere for you to have your chickens. I know it's not what you are used to, but we need a start together, even if we have already been married nearly two and a half years! Look Season in front of you there is a kitchen and we have two other downstairs rooms and two rooms upstairs" Ned was excited and keen to show me everything,

"But Ned how are we to save money when you have rented this place?" I asked, He looked a little sheepish,

"I sort of made a decision without telling you," I raised my eyebrows as if to say do you ever tell me anything. "I'm the only one they have told but Flora and Jasper are getting married, and they will be living with us and that will make the rent cheaper than the other place. I hope you don't mind, I know you have been used to your own space, but we can each have a living area and a bedroom and share the kitchen." He gazed at me biting his lip just a little waiting for my response.

"Ned I am so pleased to be with you that I don't care if I share with the whole of London. It is wonderful that Flora and Jasper have found each other."

"But the plan still is that eventually we will have a place back in the countryside, Season, it's my dream, but having you here with me will make it a whole lot easier"

I can't pretend that living in London was easy, but I grew accustomed to it. The wonky house as I referred to it was on a busy street, but a brisk walk from it was a sort of green area, not exactly a park but something to remind me of the countryside. Flora and Jasper got married, quietly without fuss just like I did with Ned. My chickens were kept in the back courtyard and the houses we shared it with didn't seem to mind although eggs frequently went missing but the birds were left alone. It was a little way from Jasper, Ned and Flora's workplace but it was cheaper than the other place and sharing the rent did help and the coins sewn into my dress weighed it down which made us feel we were accomplishing something. Jasper was unhappy that Flora had to work as a married woman but money was not in abundance so she had to bring in her share. Flora secured me a position in the laundry although I did pick up some other work once knowledge of my midwifery skills came out, although it was difficult to get the herbs and roots I needed to help with labour pains, we managed and we were all very happy.

CHAPTER TWELVE

"Ned I have to tell you something" I said as he came in from a particularly long day at the stables. He sat down and I served him some pottage from the cauldron and a hunk of bread.

"Yes darling" he said and pulled me down on his knee nearly upsetting his bowl. He dipped his bread in the pottage "What little gems of knowledge are you going to impart today?" he gave me a pottagy grin.

"Just the news that around next April or May I'm not sure yet, you will be holding our baby in your arms." I looked into his face. His last wife and baby died within days of the birth. Silence, then he jumped up and as I was on his knee I stumbled, then he took my hands and danced with me around the room.

"Season" his eyes filled with tears, "It's wonderful news. I never thought I would have another chance at fatherhood, such happiness" Relief washed through me, he was as elated as I was.

It was around January of 1533 that I had cause to revisit part of my life which I thought was long since closed. I had been working in the laundry and had reason to deliver some linens to a part of the court where I didn't usually go. I got lost, so many doorways and passageways and I knew I was in the wrong part when a group of very well dressed ladies came round the corner all chattering and gossiping, I moved to the side and bowed my head and turned to the wall knowing I shouldn't be there and then a voice, an unmistakable voice, "Season Cobb, what a surprise!" I looked up and there flanked by six ladies, standing with elegance, poise and ultimate supremacy stood Queen Anne Boleyn. I felt myself quiver and had to recover myself, I turned and Anne then saw my swollen belly and she gasped, "Why Season you have grown so fat" the other ladies giggled and sniggered. Anne looked down at the front of her gown "As you can see I am in the same state although you look a little further along than me or were just fatter to begin with?" Enjoying her moment in front of her ladies Anne just couldn't stop.

"It is predicted by everyone, I am carrying a boy, a future King" said Anne smugly. I found my voice,

"You will have a girl the same as me" said I matter-of-factly, I had no way of knowing but at this moment I wanted her to think I knew much more than I was telling. I heard the ladies gasp and they glanced at each other. An icy response from Queen Anne ,

"There is nothing the same for us. Do not flatter yourself, I am a Queen with position and power, beauty, intelligence and", at this point she approached me and curled her fingers around the leather thong which held the pearl that Ned had given me around my neck, she pulled at the necklace, jerking my face towards her "and jewels, lots of them" she sneered "You, are a fat, ungracious servant girl who will amount to nothing and I could have you cast out as easy as blinking, take care how you address me".

I remembered our dear Queen Katherine, she had cast her out, I had no doubts that I could follow, but I could not hold my tongue, it was as if someone was talking through me, the words which came out of my mouth were not of my forming. "Your Grace" at this Anne smirked, she was expecting a humbling apology and turned her back on me to re-join her group. "You will have a girl child, who will be as great as any King. It matters not how many people you have paid to tell you or our great King Henry that you will deliver of a boy. It will be a girl". Anne spun around eyes wide, her beautiful gown swayed around her, her face was deathly white. Her countenance forgotten and the feral cat quality came through,
"I will get what I want, I have prayed and God will not deny me. Get out of my sight, I will not look upon you again" Her ladies looked at her in astonishment, she had let her guard fall and they saw what the real Anne was like.

I left, my heart was pounding, I was angry, I felt unsettled. I never told Ned as I just wanted to forget about it. Whatever made me say it, how do I know if she is carrying a boy or girl, how do I know what I am carrying?

Luckily I didn't encounter Anne again and in the May of 1533, when my time came I had an easy birth, relatively quickly, attended by just Flora and an older lady who lived in one of the houses that shared the courtyard at the back of our house. My beautiful daughter was laid in my arms and I felt such love as I never thought possible. I couldn't stop studying her. I had seen so many babies but none as wonderful as my own. Ned couldn't wait to hold her and I couldn't envisage ever being this happy again.

Queen Anne gave birth in the September of that year, her laying in was the most sumptuous affair, she was attended by many women and she was rewarded with a girl just as I had prophesied. According to the gossip she was completely enamoured with her child although obviously disappointed that it wasn't a boy. Ned said the King had said the child was well favoured, I didn't really understand what that meant and that she was a "Fine Tudor". Apparently the King actually inquired as to our child, which Ned was delighted about and they talked about how lovely it was to be a father to daughters.

My life with Ned and my daughter was incredibly happy and I was very content. It worked well as there was always somebody available to look after her when I couldn't actually take her with me. Everybody loved her, she was such a good and easy child. The time passed quickly when I was around her, however I wondered how did I fill my time before I had her?

Ned would come back from court with gossip but with men they never get all the details and the year after our girls were born, Anne miscarried of a boy child. Even though I could never ever warm to Anne she must have been distraught for such an event, and our poor King had another disappointment to deal with.

Although busy I would still work at the laundry and I was asked on occasion to attend to people at the stables who had learned of my skills from Ned, so I was well known about the lesser parts of the working court. I was waiting for Ned with our daughter in the courtyard of the stables. I was pointing out the horses and animals and generally amusing my little one when a fancy carriage pulled into the yard. The person who alighted after much fuss made my heart sink. Queen Anne appeared holding a little lapdog which was thrashing about and would not keep still. Anne kept teasing it and it wasn't enjoying the experience at all. Anne lifted her head and her first look was directly at me. Her gaze made my blood run cold. Immediately the act was put on, as she was aware that she would be watched. "Season how lovely that you are here to greet me, I was hoping I would get to see you again," she said with a simpering smile. What could she mean, I no more wished to see her than she me. She turned around and excused herself from her companion who was also riding in the carriage, but she kept hold of the dog who was wriggling and yelping to be set free and approached me. She

111

then gestured to me to walk with her. My heart pounded and I looked around for help. Ned appeared just at that very moment and an excited babble from the babe startled the dog and as the baby outstretched her arms towards Ned the dog snapped at her and caught her small hand. She screamed, the dog barked and wriggled free so he was dropped to the ground. Blood poured from her hand so much so that I could not see how badly she was hurt. Ned immediately grabbed her from me and tried to comfort her whilst I looked at her hand. There was a raw gash on her little finger which was deep and I put her finger in my mouth whilst we fumbled to find something to tie around it. We were totally immersed in what we were doing and then a voice cut through the chaos, "What a lovely daughter Season." Anne stood there waiting, not helping, not caring, she obviously wasn't going to leave. "It's just a little scratch she may have a scar but it won't matter, it's not as if it will make any difference to her, it's not as if she needs her hands to look nice, she won't ever have any jewelled rings to go on them and besides little Purkoy didn't mean it" she picked up the dog and rubbed her nose on the top of his head, showing she thought more of that dog than she did of my little girl. No apology for the dog, no concern at all for my daughter, I just couldn't stop myself,

"Just like the less than perfect hand you have then" and I looked directly at her misshapen fingernail. This hit a nerve and she hurriedly hid her hand behind her skirt and looked round to see if anyone had heard the remark.

"I'll take her home" said Ned sternly, cuddling the babe and kissing her tear stained face. "Find out what the Queen wants" the disgust he felt at the Queen Anne at that moment all over his face.

"Put some chamomile and honey on her finger and bind it gently, I won't be long" I called to him wanting to go along with him. By this time there were several people just watching us and muttering so I tried to make it seem as normal as possible.

"Leave us" Anne said to all that were around, her companion then kept a modest way behind us and we walked through one of the doorways. Anne did not speak until we had approached a nook in one of the passageway walls, she then gave the reason for this mysterious liaison. "I have need of your services again. You have served me well in the past with my little problems, you saved me from the sickness and I know your skills with herbs and suchlike." What a relief that was, she just wanted a draft, but why didn't she ask her apothecary or doctor? My relief was short lived as she then said, "I need you to conjure up a medicine to beget me a healthy boy child, I need you say one of your charms to bring it true. I need to have a prince in order to secure the King's love for me. Season, last year I lost a baby boy and it has nearly destroyed me." Looking into her face I would have thought I would see anguish and pain for the child she lost but instead I saw terror, she was scared, this was about saving her own skin.

"It is not possible for me to do this" I started to say I was hardly in the mood to help this woman,

"Don't tell me that, you said that before but you still did help bring on my courses. What incantations you spoke worked. Then I was just a maid, now I ask you as your Queen. Failure this time will result in my misfortune, and I will not suffer alone".

"You have access to every kind of help, why do you need me?" I said with a shrug acting much braver than I actually was. Her voice changed and became more like a hiss. She looked over her shoulder at the companion and then moved closer to me,

"Listen, you annoying little wench I have prayed but to no avail, I cannot ask anyone here as it would go straight back to the King, so I need assistance from another source, and you are a witch. I've always known it. You must have put a spell on that husband of yours because no one else would ever have looked at you. He had to suffer your ugliness to beget a child. I was frightened of what you could do to me before but now you have a child, you have to be so careful, just think Purkoy could have bitten her face." The threat held in the air, she stepped back observing my expression of horror and she smirked, a cruel, cold, vicious look and there was venom in her eyes, even now when she wished my help she couldn't help being vindictive.

She thinks I'm a witch went through my mind, if this wasn't so serious it would be funny. "Well?" she said cocking her head to the side. Anyone watching would think she was just asking an opinion on something.

Thinking quickly, I said, "What I was going to say before you unleased your rage on me was, it is not possible for me to do this at the moment as the ingredients I need are not readily available to me. I have not funds to purchase them. I will also need a way to meet you to tell how to administer them. She nodded and it was as if the charm returned to her, she raised her voice

"Your purse quickly" she said to the companion and they did not dare object, it was given to her and then she waved them away. She gave the purse directly to me without looking inside to see what money it contained and then looked expectantly at me waiting for the next instruction.

"Have someone waiting here a week today, they will have to bring me directly to you. It will be in the evening but I cannot tell you a time so they will have to wait from dusk onwards" I said.

"I understand" she mumbled and I think she was about to walk away when she paused then asked, "What is the name of your daughter, I do hope she won't suffer any lasting damage?" I did not detect any hint of care or sympathy in the question and remembering how unkind and spiteful she was I dispensed some meanness of my own,

"She is named for a great Queen" I smiled. Anne's face turned to pure radiance and she returned my smile as graciously as I had ever seen her, she turned on her charisma but it was wasted on me. I let her have her moment of self adoration thinking I had named my daughter after her before I said "Her name is Katherine." In an instant Anne's face hardened and her lips soured into a hard line, she almost spat her next words, "She was never your Queen, you would do well to remember that". Clearly shaken Anne visibly composed herself before walking off, her aide trotting off behind her clearly wondering what it had all been about.

At this moment in time I wished I was a witch, if I'd been one I could have solved this situation. My stomach churned, my pride had put Katherine in danger. I could not magic a pregnancy or determine it to be a boy. When I returned to Ned he was still angry but when he saw my face he realised it was better not to ask any questions. He would not be pleased by my actions.

I visited several apothecaries and managed to purchase some mandrake root, it was so expensive just for a little but it was the only thing I could think of and there was more than enough money in the purse. My mother had told me it had magical powers to enable conception, but I really didn't know how to prepare it. I questioned the apothecary but I don't think he was any wiser than me and he was suspicious of my intent and the amount of money I had in my purse so I dare not draw further attention to myself.

I also had a secret of my own, I found that I was again with child. This should have been a happy time but now Anne overshadowed my joy. I did not tell Ned, wishing to tell him when the current situation had hopefully gone away.

The day came to visit Anne and I did not keep her waiting. I was at the stables just after dusk and saw a lady waiting for me, wearing a cloak which covered her face, as I approached her, she moved the hood back and it was Mistress Mary!

"Mistress Mary" I exclaimed,

"Hush Season lets go!. Anne didn't trust anyone else so she sent me, she's really desperate Season. Do you think it will work?" I couldn't answer Mary and all the time we were hurrying along with Mary glancing around her anxiously so as not to be seen. We went up a staircase and along a gallery and through a hidden door to Anne's chamber, surprisingly there was very little security on this route, just a sleepy page by the entrance to the staircase.

Anne sat by her fire with her sewing on her lap, but she was gazing into the flames with a very sad, forlorn look. Hearing the door she turned her head and the pale, worried face stared at me with much hope. There were no pleasantries between us, I was straight to the point. I handed over the prepared posset containing the mandrake root, mixed with something to make her relax, herbs and spices which may or may not help. My instructions were for her to take it every night for seven days and then seven days after that she would need to couple with the King as many times as they were able. She nodded. I told her that I would be also chanting incantations as she had called them in order to entice the right outcome.

I couldn't let the occasion pass without extracting some revenge for myself. I told Anne that in order that she become pregnant she would have to pray for a past trouble of hers. For her to accept blame and take the responsibility of her actions. She nodded, eager to do anything. I then told her she needed to pray for Thomas More who had died on the executioner's block because he would not acknowledge Anne as Queen because this was contradictory to his beliefs and he believed the King's marriage to Queen Katherine was valid. I told Anne she needed to pray with an uplifted heart and genuine feeling for the soul of Thomas More. I will say that she was an accomplished actress and her face remained calm although I cannot imagine the inner torment of having to do so and admit her mistake to herself and to God.

I took my leave. Mistress Mary saw me back to familiar territory. That night and every night for seven nights I wished over the bones. I knew wishing for something good to come to someone I absolutely detested would not work, so I wished for the next child born of the King would be a healthy boy. I wore the sleeves the King gave me, I chanted over the bones and I rubbed my stomach, hoping the fact that I was with child would be some extra help, especially as no one was aware of it. On the seventh night I buried the bones in the back courtyard. I was exhausted and I had no way of knowing if anything would work.

CHAPTER THIRTEEN

My baby is due at the end of next month. I feel unwell with this child. Sickness which did not plague me with Katherine does not want to leave me this time. My own concoctions have helped but I have promised to further my knowledge in this area and hopefully alleviate this woozy feeling. I blame myself for wishing for a baby for Anne on my growing belly those months ago.

I received a purse with many coins in payment for Anne's pregnancy. Two months after my intervention Mistress Mary informed me that Anne was pregnant. I was amazed that it had worked. I believe it was the fact that Anne thought it would work, stopped worrying, calmed herself and nature worked its own magic. She was sure this was a boy child and all hopes rested on it. I kept the coins, we had enough with what Ned had been saving for years to start anew, with our dream of a house in the countryside. As I was so close to birthing the new babe we had decided to wait until after the birth before we left. On Ned's travels he had seen a patch of land and a tumble-down building which was just within our financial reach, far away from anyone who knew us. Every day I wished for my baby and our new life.

Katherine's wound healed nicely but there would always be a scar which ran down the inside of her little finger. Every time I looked at it, it brought forth reminders of that day and that horrible dog and the way Anne seemed to enjoy the injury it had caused to my sweet little girl. I wished ill on that dog. I wished grief on Anne.

Since Anne became pregnant she had left us alone so when a frenzied, unaccompanied Mistress Mary came by carriage to my wonky house one morning in middle January 1536 I was bewildered. "You must come Season," tears were pouring from her eyes, "Anne needs you." she was grabbing at my arm trying to drag me to the carriage. Ned appeared behind me at the door and Mistress Mary looked surprised, she had clearly thought I would be on my own.

"Mistress Mary," Ned inclined his head as he said the greeting. "Season you cannot go anywhere, you are too close to your time." he said to me although I felt the content was directed at Mistress Mary.

"Season I beg you, Anne needs you, we cannot ask anyone else, she is losing the child! Since last night she has been trying to hold on but I fear she is now losing her mind as well as the child".

"I'm sorry but Season cannot go with you. You will have to get assistance from somewhere else" Ned put his hand on my arm and tried to gently bring me back into the house.

"Season, I am asking you please. I have never asked you for anything but she is my sister and in spite of her failings I love her dearly, please" the expression on her tear stained face softened my resolve. I looked at Ned,

"I'm sorry darling but I must go." Ned was not happy, he looked at me and Mistress Mary and back to me.

"Mistress Mary, I am charging you to see Season safety back to me, but watch her too. I do not like this at all and keep that blasted dog away from her too".

"Oh the dog won't bother you, it jumped through a window to its death a month or so ago, Anne was devastated. The King had to deliver the news himself as no one else could do it with Anne in her condition. Then the King had a fall whilst out hunting and they told Anne he was dead and I think that has caused the baby to come. Please, please come quickly, please." Mary was begging now and becoming quite incoherent. I went into the house to collect my bag. I felt pains myself but they were early signs so I knew I had a day or so before I would be ready. I had not told Ned as he would have worried and he definitely would not have let me go with Mistress Mary.

The sight of Anne laying on her bed, with a wax-like complexion, sweating, crying and hysterical reminded me of those years ago when she had the sweating sickness. If only I was sure the outcome of this would be as positive. Anne lay with blood over her legs and nightgown and deep down I knew it was already too late. When I went to her she grabbed my arm, "Whatever you want Season it's yours just deliver me of a healthy son."

It was swift, the delivery of a very small son of about 6 months in the belly. The pain of the birth was nothing to the lamentation of Anne when the child did not breathe. He looked perfect, but he did not take air, and I tried, whilst Anne wrung her hands and rocked herself back and forth. Mary stood like a statue just staring at the babe. "Anne, I'm so sorry" I said, like those words could make her feel any better, then she looked at me and at that moment I doubled up in pain. Then another pain ripped through me and I felt warm liquid running down my inner thighs. No, no, not now my baby was coming and it wasn't going to wait! I cried out I just couldn't help it and Mary looked at me. I crumbled to my knees clutching at my swollen belly. "I need to get home to Ned" I said,

"You are going nowhere, you know you would never get there, your baby is being born now Season!" Mary had regained her senses and put aside her concerns for her sister and was focusing on me. Anne continued to stare into space and rock back and forth cradling her dead son. Mary helped me to the pallet at the side of Anne's bed. Each pain was ripping through me so much more intensely than they had with Katherine. The urge to push was strong, but not here, it wasn't right, not with a dead child in the room and the mother needing care of her own. Another scream and I knew it was coming. I felt down and could feel the head. Surely someone would hear and come thinking it was the Queen? I gripped the bed post and pulled myself onto my knees and hoped the weight of the baby would help pull itself from me. All the time Mary was attending me, cooling my forehead with scented water, offering words of encouragement, rubbing my back. One huge horrendous push which I know tore me open and a baby slid out and was caught by Mary. I slumped down, exhausted and breathless. Mary stood holding a bloody, wet, blue child and was gazing at me. When my fuzzy brain realised that the child was not breathing I grabbed at it and opened its mouth, it was full of mucus, its tiny nose was filled with fluid, I cleared the child, I rubbed the child and prayed hard and I was rewarded by just the faintest noise like the sound of a tiny kitten. Such relief as I had ever known. My son was alive!. Mary handed me a blanket and I wrapped him tightly, thankful to feel his warm little body. I laid with him for only a few minutes when I got the pain which delivered the afterbirth.

I put the child down next to me and Mary turned her back to get some water and a cloth for me to wash with. Mary was saying, "Season, you cannot stay here you must go now. If anyone should find out about the Queen. As soon as you can you need to get away from here. I know it's unfair but let's get you sorted quickly"

She was quick, I didn't see her, Mary didn't see her but Anne was holding my child. Her own she had discarded and he was laying on the floor uncovered. "Anne" Mary moved towards her but Anne backed away, clutching my son to her.

"Name your price Season. Anything you desire can be yours."

"Anne, put the baby down" said Mary as gently as she could. "Let us clean you up Anne" she put out her hand as if to touch the baby and Anne snatched back and the child squealed. My throat was dry and fear was swirling within me. She wasn't in her right mind. I just stood there watching every move.

"Do you want jewels Season, as many as you can see, do you want a position at court, a title, I can arrange that and you can wear beautiful dresses? Do you want your own house and servants, it can all be yours?" Anne circled me all the time stroking the head of my son and kissing the top of his head gently.

"Anne, give Season the baby" said Mary, I noticed she said the baby not my baby, she was unsure of how Anne would react.

"Did you want to be my son's wet nurse?" Anne said, obviously thinking this could be an answer. "You would never go hungry again and your daughter just think what you could give her, do for her. The King would never know. You can easily have another child to replace this one" She thought she could buy my baby and deceive the King, she thought I would give up my child and birth another to replace it, just like that, could this woman sink any further in life? The baby, my son, then started to make a noise, a retching sound. I looked in horror at Anne and she, in absolute terror, down at the baby.

"Anne, give him to Season, he's ailing, he needs attention!" screamed Mary. I, who had been standing uselessly by then found some courage,

"He will choke, Anne give him to me, I will see to him". Amazingly, there must have been a motherly instinct in her and Anne handed over the baby. I grabbed him. Anne stood with her hands over her mouth, eyes wide. I turned my back and looked at my son, it was nothing just further mucus which had just come up, but I did not let on. Mary had opened the door to the chamber and I knew I had to make my escape. I bolted to the door clutching the baby to my chest. Before Anne knew what was happening I was through it and running down the gallery, down the stairs. I heard the door close behind me and I think Mary was barring Anne from following as I could hear heated exchanges. The baby, bless him, was quiet as if he knew the danger we were in and as I reached familiar sights in the stable yard I saw my beloved Ned with Katherine and some hastily fetched possessions on a cart. Blood was pouring from my body from the tear after giving birth, I felt panic but seeing Ned was so welcome, and I offered up the baby to him and climbed into the cart even though the pain seared through me.

"I knew all was not well, and I just had a feeling" he said the worried look ageing his face, "We are starting our new life together tonight. I thought to just rescue you but you have brought me another child!" Ned said with wonder.

"It's our son Ned. She tried to steal him, to buy him, she wanted me to give him up, she" I was hysterical and now in floods of tears and I felt his comforting arm around me. My darling little Katherine put her little hand out to grasp mine and it was all too much for my mind and my body and I sobbed with pain, and fear and relief all at once. Ned was drawing the cart out of the yard when the sleepy page from the bottom of the staircase ran to the cart and threw something up at him, which landed at his feet. Without looking he just picked it up and tucked it in his tunic, and we turned away from that place, from her and left.

Much later we looked at what the boy had thrown. It was a purse of money and a note from Mary. Between Ned and myself we managed to decipher the content,

"Dearest Season,

Take your family and go far away from here. This place is corrupt and evil and Anne is consumed by it. She will not rest until she gets what she thinks is owed to her. I bear you no ill feeling, I envy that you can disappear, and I wish I could. I am not wealthy in my own right, I have to rely on Anne, so take this small sum and use it for your family.

I am grateful to you.

Mary"

EPILOGUE

I would never forgive Anne.

Anne's fall from grace was quick, once the magic of the relationship with King Henry floundered, she lost all those things which she thought were important and her good looks and clever tongue did not save her. His Grace the King saw the Anne we could all see. It has been said that she had bewitched him for seven years but now he had broken the spell. She was due to be executed on May 18th but I wished on the bones for the suffering to last just a little longer after all the pain she caused me and the swordsman's journey to

England was delayed by weather. I never wanted to see her again but a small part of me wished I could have witnessed her end. I hope she finds forgiveness for only God can give that.

I never thought of myself as a witch, my mother did used to say that we needed to be careful as curing of ailments and brewing of potions could be construed as witchcraft if interpreted wrongly. Am I a witch? I leave that to you to decide. In the meantime I live very happily with my husband, son and daughter in the country.

AUTHORS NOTE

Season Cobb is fictitious she never existed but she has been a character in my head for years and I thought it time for her to make an appearance on paper.

The Boleyn family did exist and many stories have been told about them and apart from hard facts we do not know what sort of people they really were.

I believe Anne Boleyn was manipulated by her family to further their own ambitions and I think she had more spirit that Henry VIII's other wives which ultimately caused her downfall. I personally feel that she wasn't as bad as the books, films and myself have indicated.

Thank you for reading my first attempt at writing, I hope I have woven a tale which will amuse, intrigue and perhaps inspire others to find out about this fascinating period in history.

BIBLIOGRAPHY

The Tudor Housewife by Alison Sim

Henry VIII King & Court by Alison Weir

The Queens of Henry VIII by David Starkey

Mary Boleyn by Alison Weir

Anne Boleyn by Joanna Denny

The Six Wives of Henry VIII by Alison Weir

VNR Colour Dictionary of Herbs and Herbalism by
Malcolm Stuart

ACKNOWLEDGMENTS

I would like to thank Angela Warwick for giving me both the inspiration and motivation with this project. Without you Angela this would not have happened.

To Mum and Dad for introducing me to history at a very young age and who encouraged me to learn and absorb every inch of it even if I did make them visit every castle I could find!

To my sister Stephanie who shares in my fascination with history and who has always been someone I look up to.

Son Aaron and partner Wayne just for being there.

A special mention to my Nanny, although you are no longer with us, visiting your garden full of fruit bushes, flowers, plants and herbs and hearing all about them and how they could be used, a stimulus and a seed planted in a young mind.

To all those others, you know who you are, thank you all so much for your support and valued wisdom.

Printed in Poland
by Amazon Fulfillment
Poland Sp. z o.o., Wrocław

53160902R10087